"What happened to that trust, Thad?"

Vanessa's words were a challenge. Abruptly Thad released her, his face hard, eyes glittering coldly.

"It came up against some hard facts," he said, "and eventually—shattered."

"It must have been very fragile. Like your love."

His jaw tightened. "Be careful what you say, Vanessa. It wouldn't take much to make me—"

"What?" she taunted. "Hit me? It couldn't hurt much more than what you've been doing to me over the past few months, with your idiotic suspicion, and your—your so-called lovemaking. Because whatever it was that you were making, it certainly wasn't love!"

Even now, as their eyes blazed antagonism and distrust at each other, the nearness of him acted like a drug on her senses, and her breath quickened....

Other titles by

DAPHNE CLAIR

IN HARLEQUIN PRESENTS

Other titles by

DAPHNE CLAIR

IN HARLEQUIN ROMANCES

DAPHNE CLAIR

something less than love

Harlequin Books

TORONTO • LONDON • NEW YORK • AMSTERDAM
SYDNEY • HAMBURG • PARIS • STOCKHOLM

Harlequin Presents edition published July 1980
ISBN 0-373-10367-0

Original hardcover edition published in 1979
by Mills & Boon Limited

Printed in U.S.A.

CHAPTER ONE

VANESSA walked up the broad steps to the hospital doorway with a strange mixture of excitement and trepidation which gave her a slightly nauseated feeling in her stomach.

Thad was coming home today—coming home after long months of pain and anxiety, hopes and fears that had changed both of them and put a strain on their relationship that at times became almost intolerable. If the accident that had occurred so shortly after their married life began had left its visible mark on her husband, it had also marked Vanessa in more subtle, not easily defined ways. She was slimmer than she had been, for one thing, her lovely figure verging on thinness. Her face had fined down, too, the cheekbones less well covered, giving her beauty a distinction that mere prettiness never achieved. Even her hair had darkened several shades and was no longer golden blonde; she had spent less time outdoors than usual lately, spending every possible moment with Thad in the hospital while he was very ill, and later taking a job in a bank, partly to ease their financial situation, and partly to give herself something else to think about when she was away from Thad.

A man coming out of the main door held it open for her and she smiled her thanks, barely noticing the appreciative glance he cast over her as she passed him. She made for the lift around the corner automatically, the hospital layout as familiar to her now as her own home, and as the doors slid closed behind her she tightened her grip on the overnight bag and silently prayed that things would get back to normal, now that Thad was well again.

When she stepped out of the lift and walked to the ward doors, she could see herself reflected in the glass there—the blue suit which matched her eyes looking trim over a blouse printed with tiny forget-me-nots, fair hair smooth and tidy in its chignon. She looked cool and competent and perhaps a little older than her twenty-four years, she thought.

He was waiting for her when she walked into the room, sitting up in the bed that he always managed to rumple ten minutes after the nurses had tidied it for him, his dark head turned to the door as she came through it, equally dark eyes watching her walk towards him across the polished vinyl floor, making her strangely nervous.

Vanessa put the bag on the chair by his bed and bent to kiss him, experiencing a familiar stirring of uneasiness at the unresponsive touch of his lips. Not for the first time, she told herself that the presence of three other men in the shared room was enough to make even Thad diffident about showing affection too openly.

As she straightened he turned his head a little away from her, towards the window, so that the scar that began on his forehead and marred the line of his left eyebrow, then slashed across his cheek, was almost hidden from her. The plastic surgery they had done after the major repairs to his broken bones and torn flesh had not been totally effective. He was lucky to have the use of his right eye, although the vision was slightly impaired. The broken bones in his leg, that had shattered in several places, had knitted perfectly, according to the doctors, and the severed tendons which had threatened to paralyse his right hand had been repaired and were responding very well to physiotherapy.

'I've brought your clothes,' Vanessa said, breaking the heavy silence that followed her greeting. She began unpacking them and laying them on the bed. 'Sister said we can go just as soon as you're ready.'

He hadn't moved, and, feeling slightly perplexed, she turned to draw the curtains about the bed, the green folds shutting them both in. Then she turned back to the bed and began to pick up the freshly ironed shirt she had brought for him.

Curtly, he said, 'I don't need help, Vanessa. I'm not crippled, and I'm not a child, either.'

'Of course not,' she said, dropping the shirt back on the bed. The astonishing fact dawned on her that he didn't want to dress in front of her, and almost unable to believe it, she said, 'Shall I wait—outside?'

'Please.'

As she closed the curtain again behind her, she was almost tempted to laugh. Surely Thad was not being motivated by *modesty*? They had been married for two weeks before the accident happened, after all, and he had shown no qualms *then* about dressing or undressing in front of her—and a public hospital was hardly the place to induce a man to become shy about such things.

Of course, before the accident his body had been almost unmarked, only a small scar or two left over from boyhood adventures marring the smoothness of its texture over hard bone and muscle. Vanessa had never tried to hide her pleasure in the feel of him, her delight in looking at him when they made love, and afterwards in the sweet languorous moments when they lay together softly touching and stroking and murmuring intimate compliments to each other.

Now his body as well as his face was scarred, and one part of her wept inwardly for that, for the spoiling of something which had been aesthetically beautiful in its way—like a picture irreparably damaged—but even deeper was her love for Thad, for every part of him, marred or perfect. The marks on his face and body could only make her love him more, if that was possible, because he had received them for her—protecting her from the inevitable crash when he had done all in his power to avoid it, and could do nothing more. When the truck which had seemed to appear from nowhere slewed on to the wrong side of the road and loomed in front of their car, in the final moments he had thrown himself sideways in a frantic effort to shield Vanessa.

He had largely succeeded. Her injuries had been superficial and quickly healed. She began to suspect that his had been worse, in a way, than anyone had realised. Thad had always been a good-looking young man, with a slightly flamboyant male charm that drew attention to his tall, virile physique and the undeniable attraction of his tanned skin. Thad Nelson's success with girls had never been in doubt, and in fact when he had first tried to convince Vanessa that he was serious about her, she had been afraid to believe him, afraid of becoming another in a line of girls he had made lighthearted love to before moving on to fresh fields of conquest.

Women were supposed to be more sensitive to physical disfigurement than men, Vanessa mused. But perhaps men were just better than women at covering up their feelings—and perhaps a man like Thad, with his quite striking good looks impaired, would be more sensitive than most.

A soft smile curved her lips as she promised herself to show him that nothing could diminish his attraction for her. It shouldn't be hard ... Tonight, when at last they were in their own small home, the home they had been heading for the night of the disastrous accident that had so radically altered their lives, she would show him—she would find every scar that marked the measure of his love for her, and kiss it ...

Sudden desire shook her even at the thought, and she bit her lip, feeling her cheeks colour as she turned blindly to stare out the window, away from the curious looks of the three men in the other beds.

The rings of the curtain around the bed rattled as Thad pulled them impatiently back, and she turned to look at him, wondering if he could read her feelings in her face. He had once been very good at that, when she had felt the way she did now ...

But the face he turned to her was hard and shuttered, the dark eyes looking a little narrowed, perhaps because she was standing in front of the window, against the light. He looked like a stranger, in his clothes, and she said, 'It must feel strange, being dressed after all this time.'

She moved towards him, and he turned and picked up the bag from the bed. Vanessa said, 'Your things——' And he said shortly, 'I've put everything in here. Let's go.'

He said goodbye to the other men, and they wished him luck and made jokes as he and Vanessa left. She wanted to take his arm, but he seemed to be walking deliberately a little way from her and when she moved closer to him, in some imperceptible way he managed to maintain the distance.

The ward Sister was waiting by the door at the end of the long corridor and Thad stopped to hold out his hand and thank her.

'Well, Mr Nelson, you've had a long stay,' she said.

'We'll miss you, but no doubt your wife will be glad to have you home again.'

'I certainly will!' Vanessa said feelingly, and Thad shot her an odd look that was almost mocking, the smile that touched his mouth leaving his nearly black eyes unamused.

'Look after him,' the Sister said. 'Don't let him try to do too much all at once. He'll still need to take it easy for a while.'

'I will!' Vanessa promised, speaking as much to Thad as to the woman. As they left the ward and went towards the lift she determinedly put her hand through his arm, saying, 'It *will* be lovely to have you home, darling! Aren't you glad?'

'Of course. I don't suppose anyone relishes the thought of spending a lifetime in hospital.'

It wasn't the answer she had expected, and it slightly chilled her, increasing the feeling of unease that had been creeping over her for some weeks. As the elevator bore them to the ground floor, she told herself that he must be feeling strange after so long a time in hospital, perhaps even a bit nervous of leaving it, after depending on it for his life; for months it had been the only home he knew.

Trying to act as normally as possible, she smiled up at him on their way to the car park. 'I talk about your coming home, but I wonder if it feels like home to you. You've never lived there, have you? You know, I hated going there, the first time—after the accident, I mean. We had made so many plans together, and we should have arrived together, when our honeymoon was over—settled in to being an old married couple—do you remember joking about it?'

'Does it feel like home to you?' he asked.

'No,' she said. 'Not without you. But it's been nice to sleep there sometimes—with all the things around me that we put there together. They're still there, Thad, still waiting ...'

As I have, her heart added. It had been such a long, anxious wait—and now Thad was at last coming home. And she wished she could shake off the dreadful feeling that something was not quite right.

She looked up at her husband's face, to find him giving her an oddly sharp look that puzzled her. 'What is it?' she asked involuntarily.

He looked away, then said, 'Nothing. Is that the car? I'd almost forgotten the other was a write-off.'

'Yes,' Vanessa said, surprised. 'How did you know?'

'I recognised Cornflake,' he said, nodding to the miniature kangaroo that dangled on the inside of the windscreen. Vanessa had brought the little mascot back from her trip across the Tasman to Australia, where she had lived for two years before coming back to her native New Zealand and becoming engaged to Thad. 'Not another of those things in the world,' said Thad drily, 'has two left-facing ears and a tail that droops on the end.'

'He may not be beautiful,' Vanessa said, 'but I love him.'

'As a mascot, he's fairly useless,' Thad reminded her. 'Did you dig him out of the wreckage?'

'The garage people did. And what do you mean, he's useless? We both survived, didn't we?'

'It's the way you look at things, I guess,' said Thad, watching her unlock the car door and slide into the driver's seat. He went round to the other side and got in beside her, throwing the bag on to the rear seat and pulling forward his safety-belt to do it up.

It was more than an hour's drive to the little township of Aputa, most of the way through farming country, once they were clear of Auckland's thriving suburbs, a task made easy by the motorway that was accessible not far from the hospital.

The hills rolled away before them, the road streaking over their gentle contours, and Vanessa could see Thad looking interestedly at the green fields with their sprinklings of sheep and cattle, the neat farmhouses, many of them brick, these days, and the occasional patches of native bush that still remained in a few of the deep folds in the landscape.

'It must seem all very—strange to you,' she said.

'It is an odd feeling,' he agreed. 'Do you know we seem to me to be going incredibly fast?'

Immediately Vanessa's foot left the accelerator, as, horrified, she exclaimed, 'Of course! You haven't been in a car since——'

'Don't be ridiculous,' he said. 'I'm not terrified, just interested that I seem to have lost my sense of speed altogether. I checked the speedometer ages ago, and I know perfectly well you weren't a millimetre over the speed limit.'

She looked at him, and he didn't look at all perturbed, only faintly amused. 'You're sure you're not—nervous?' she said. '*I* was, the first time I drove again.'

'I'm not nervous,' he said with faint irritation. 'As for driving—I'll find out about that when I come to it, won't I?'

He returned to looking out at the passing countryside,

and Vanessa pressed on the accelerator and brought the speed up swiftly again to eighty kilometres per hour. She felt bleak and vaguely hurt, and told herself that the move from hospital to home would be a strain on Thad's equilibrium, accounting for his apparently uncertain temper, and on hers too. Perhaps she was over-reacting, anyway. She had been looking forward to this day so long, the actual event was inevitably anticlimactic.

She drew in to one of the fruit and vegetable stalls on the Bombay hills, to take advantage of the cheaper prices and the freshness of produce grown on the rich volcanic soil of the Pukekohe district. The Indian shopkeeper spoke with the marked accent of his homeland, but the teenage sons who helped him spoke typical New Zealand English.

She brought broccoli, because Thad was fond of it, and tomatoes because they always added colour to a meal, and tonight they were to have a special meal; and some kumeras, because the sweet potato flavour would complement the broccoli, and go well with the chicken dish she had planned. There were some late strawberries, expensive, but she bought them, too, and thought she must remember to get some cream before they reached home.

Thad had got out of the car but not come with her. Vanessa stowed her purchases in the car and looked about, seeing him standing against a fence nearby, leaning on a post and looking down across the valley below. Blue-hazed hills rose in the distance across a panorama of green intersected by farm hedges, dotted with tall trees, and with a road and a river intermittently visible, and some clusters of houses here and there.

Coming to stand beside him, she said softly, 'It's beautiful, isn't it?'

After a moment he turned his head and said, 'Yes.' But she had a strong feeling that he had not really been looking at the view.

Perhaps she was wrong, because the next thing he said, turning back to look at it, was, 'Meremere's going strong today.'

She looked at the four tall chimneys of the coal-fired power station a few miles across the valley, and said, 'Yes. Even *that* looks attractive from here—the smoke looks quite romantic, floating up into the air in that deceptively lazy fashion.'

'Romantic,' he repeated, not in a questioning fashion, but the look he turned to her was questioning. He said her name, almost under his breath, and then, 'Are you——'

Vanessa moved involuntarily closer, and then a hideous blast from a car horn made her jump, and they both turned their heads to find that another customer had found their car in his impatient way as he tried to move out of the crowded little space in front of the stall.

There was nothing for it but to hurry back to the car and apologetically move it and be on their way.

When she had picked up speed again and they were clear of the hills, she asked him, 'What were you going to say back there?'

'When? Oh—nothing. Just something about the view. I've forgotten,' Thad said.

Such a battery of conflicting excuses that she was immediately convinced he was prevaricating.

But no good would come of pressing the point, she was sure. Silently Vanessa drove on.

By the time they reached the house she felt stretched tight with nerves. Trying to act naturally, she ran the car into the garage and said, too brightly, she knew, 'Well, here we are. Welcome to your happy home, Thad—at last.'

The wry smile still missed his eyes, as he reached for the bag on the back seat and got out. Vanessa hauled out the bag of greengroceries and slammed shut the car door with her foot. She led the way up the short concrete path to the back door and put down the bag while she fumbled for the key, in her handbag. She opened the door and as she made to pick up the vegetables, Thad said, 'Leave that! I'll get it.'

He put down his overnight bag on the floor and stooped to pick up the other.

'Be careful!' Vanessa warned automatically.

Thad swung the bag on to the table and turned to her, his eyes smouldering with annoyance. 'It's not breakable, is it?'

'I meant—you,' she said, knowing that he knew it.

'*I'm* not, either,' he said. 'They wouldn't have let me leave the hospital if I was that fragile.'

'They said to be careful——'

'*All right!*' he snapped. 'I'll be careful. I don't need you fussing around *telling* me to be careful every damned time I try to do some perfectly ordinary little thing!'

Speechless herself, she stared at him, and the tension of the past couple of hours became an unbearable tightness in her chest.

More quietly, Thad said, 'I've got to get back to normal, Vanessa. I'm not an invalid, and you—you mustn't treat me like one. I didn't mean to—snarl.'

'I'm sorry,' she said. 'I suppose I was being over-protective. I'll try not to fuss again.'

He said, 'I'll take this into the bedroom,' and picked up the overnight bag, going out of the little kitchen into the hallway and towards the front bedroom they had furnished together before their wedding.

It was obvious that he didn't want her to accompany him, so she tightened her teeth against the threatening tears and began to unpack the paper bag on the table. When she had finished that, she held her head high and went firmly down the hall to the bedroom.

The door was shut. Suppressing an urge to knock on it, she opened it and walked in, saying, 'If you give me your pyjamas you had on in the hospital, I'll wash them for you tomorrow.'

He was standing by the bed, holding a bundle of letters and cards that he had evidently taken out of the bag. 'What?' he said, turning to frown at her. She saw the pyjamas with a pile of clothes on the bed, and he waved vaguely at them. 'Oh—there.'

Vanessa picked them up and said casually, 'You got quite a lot of mail, didn't you, in the hospital. What are you going to do with all those, now?'

Thad said, in a fierce undertone, 'Burn them!' And she blinked.

He turned and tossed the bundle, secured with a thick rubber band, on to the bedside table, and began to rummage in the bag for something else, taking out his toilet bag, the one he had used on their honeymoon. She must have imagined the intensity in his voice.

She picked up the bundle, saying, 'It seems a pity—I recall some rather nice cards that some people sent——' She began to ease off the rubber band, and his hand came out and wrenched the bundle out of hers.

'Weren't you ever taught not to read other people's correspondence?' he asked roughly.

Stunned, she said, 'I—wasn't intending to read it. Just

to look at the cards. At the hospital there was a notice asking for Christmas cards and the like, for the children's ward. The children make them into scrapbooks or something. I thought——'

'I'll pick out the pretty cards, and you can send them to the hospital,' he said. 'Satisfied?'

She nodded, not able to answer him, and kept her head down. She gritted her teeth, but that didn't stop a tear from falling and making a small wet mark on the pyjamas she still held clutched in her arms.

Blindly, she made a move to leave the room, but then Thad gave a soft, forceful exclamation, and his arms came round her, pulling her against him. She heard him say '*Don't cry!*' rather savagely, and she closed her eyes tightly and gritted her teeth again to keep back the tears.

Her face was against his jacket, and his arms were tight about her, and it was heaven—a heaven she had missed for too long. His face was against her hair, and she could hear his breath, feel it stirring the tendrils that had strayed against her temple, but he was tense—terribly, rigidly tense—she could feel it in every muscle.

She moved a little, nuzzling her face against him, moved until her forehead was against his throat, where the open neck of his shirt began. Her lips were brushing against the linen of his shirt, and if she opened another button, her mouth would reach a spot that she remembered well ...

She let the pyjamas drop to the carpet and moved her hand up gently to tease the button open and put her parted mouth against his slightly dampened skin. She felt him draw in a breath that made his body shudder against hers, and deliberately she moved herself closer—as close as she could get without his help.

He still didn't move, and she slid her mouth up a little,

pressing tiny kisses on his skin, until she could reach the beating pulse at the base of his throat, and delicately touch it with the tip of her tongue ...

The movement that she felt then was quite involuntary, and she looked up into his face and gave a soft laugh, and then at last his hands moved, pulling her so tightly against him that she swayed into the curve of his body as he bent over her, throwing the bundle of letters on to the bed with a soft plop that she heard but didn't register; tilting her head and holding it exactly where he wanted it while his mouth possessed, inflamed, devoured hers. Her senses telescoped and concentrated on that one thing in the universe—his mouth, then shattered in a million kaleidoscopic pieces and reformed into something else—some shivery, brilliant delight that was her and Thad and their love all coming together at last, at last in a beautiful, preordained pattern.

Everything would be all right, she thought incoherently. Everything must come right for them—their loving would dissolve the tensions and strains forged over the past months, and heal the mental scars.

His mouth hurt her, it was so fiercely passionate, and she pulled away at last, only to press more small kisses on his chin and whisper, 'Oh, Thad—oh, darling, I've missed you!' And then tip back her head as he threaded his fingers into her hair, because she knew he liked to kiss her throat, sliding his lips along her shoulders while his hands held her and his thumbs gently felt the curves of her breasts.

Today he was less gentle than ever before, but she understood that—it had been so long ...

She took his hands in hers and put them behind her, sliding her own arms about his shoulders and whispered against the curve of his jaw, 'Thad—darling—let's go to bed!'

He was looking over her shoulder, and she was almost certain that he had actually made a move to comply, to push her the few inches that would bring them both down on the inviting softness of the purple candlewick spread.

Then, incredibly, he moved his hands from their delicious hold on her and slid them up her arms to jerk her away from him. She looked up at him in incredulous astonishment, and his face was the face of a stranger. It was bitter and savagely mocking and the words he said were unbelievably, horrifyingly strange and awful.

'My, my,' he drawled. 'You really are a sex-starved little bitch, aren't you. Can't you even wait until we've eaten?'

CHAPTER TWO

SHE was stricken, standing staring at her husband in frozen disbelief and thinking, *This can't be true. It must be a nightmare.*

He turned away from her, and his foot caught in the pyjamas that lay in a forgotten heap on the floor. She saw him bend and pick them up, then he put them in her hands and said, 'You'd better take these.'

She took them, and he turned his back on her and began taking things out of the bag on the bed again. Vanessa walked to the door, her feet heavy as though she was walking in water, and she thought again, hopefully, *It's a nightmare. None of it's real.*

But it was, and somehow she had to live through this,

somehow she had to make sense out of the unbelievable.

She put the pyjamas on the small heap of clothing on top of the washing machine in the spotless little laundry, and mechanically walked back into the kitchen and began making preparations for their meal. She had worked everything out beforehand and it didn't take much thought, even though the dish was quite elaborate, with chicken and nuts and herbs and a special wine sauce concoction to go over it all.

She set the small table in the dining area with the new cloth she had bought and its matching napkins, and the plates from the lovely dinner set that her parents had given them for their wedding present, that had never been used.

When Thad left the bedroom and she saw him go into the lounge she walked quietly down the hallway, and as she turned to go into the bedroom, caught a glimpse of him standing with his hands in his pockets, looking out of the window towards the road that was just visible through the trees that bordered the section. They both loved trees, and had counted themselves lucky to have found this house with its profusion of young oaks and poplars, Australian wattles and native tarata, kowhai and manuka. They had liked the house, but loved the garden, and she remembered they had wandered about with arms entwined, planning additions to it, and mapping out a place for a future patio where they could sit on comfortable outdoor chairs and enjoy it together. Thad had kissed her in the shadow of one of the wattles, one day, and the fine powdery blossoms had dusted her hair with gold that he had brushed away with gentle fingers, teasing her lightly as he did so.

'Now I know what you use to make it that lovely colour,' he had said.

Standing in the bedroom, remembering, Vanessa could see herself in the mirror, and her hair had lost its golden glow, and her face its sheen of young happiness.

Was that why Thad had changed towards her? Did he no longer find her attractive, now that she was looking more mature, less a girl? Until this year she had always looked a few years less than her age, but now, with the worry of Thad's injuries and the grief of losing her father only a short time later, all traces of girlishness had left her face.

She stood before the mirror and slowly took out the pins that held her hair. Thad's fingers had wreaked havoc with the style anyway, when he had held her—so roughly, but surely, surely there had been desire there. With relief, she remembered there had been no doubt of it, she had *known* he wanted her, and that was why his sudden rejection had been such an incredible shock.

She did look younger with her hair down, and she began to brush it, planning to leave it loose. The dress she had planned to change into was in the wardrobe. Thad had left the door a little ajar, and she could see the soft folds of dull gold chiffon. She had worn the dress on their honeymoon, and never since. Her case had survived the crash with only a dent and a couple of scratches, and all her clothes had been safe.

Perhaps she had simply over-reacted—maybe he had meant it as a joke—a rather clumsy way of telling her he wanted to wait until later, until all the preliminary trimmings, the leisurely dinner, herself in a glamorous gown, all the celebrations of his homecoming, had been gone through. A gradual build-up to the right, longed-for moment, rather than a hasty, spontaneous explosion of passion.

Certainly he had seemed quite casual afterwards, as though he had no idea of how deeply and devastatingly he had hurt her—shocked her. Her rationalising had a hollow ring, but it was the best she could do. There had to be some sort of explanation, and it was the only one which seemed to make any sense at all. As a joke, his words had been crude and uncharacteristic, but perhaps the months in hospital had changed his views on what was funny—she had a vague notion that hospital humour tended to be earthy.

She put down the brush and decided to have a shower before she changed. Standing under the warm water, she used perfumed soap, and after towelling herself she dusted a talc with the same floral perfume over her skin, giving it a silky sheen. With a towel wrapped about her she walked out into the bedroom, pulling the plastic cap from her hair, and Thad turned from the bedside table where he had been putting something in the drawer and looked at her.

Just looked. That was all, but the blaze in his eyes was unmistakable, and she felt a surge of triumph mixed with joy. She would have gone over to him and flung her arms about his neck, offered him her warm, scented body to do as he liked with, if it hadn't been for the rebuff she had received a short time ago. Instead she stood where she was, while his eyes took in the loosened hair that hung across her bare shoulders, the damp towel that hugged her breasts, the long legs that showed beneath its edge, and travelled slowly back to her face.

Her lips parted and she almost smiled—and then his face closed like a door shutting out the sun, and he turned and walked out of the room.

Vanessa dressed slowly and with great care, putting on a hint of lipstick and a discreet amount of eye make-up to accentuate the blue of her eyes. She fastened on a pair of amber drop earrings, but just pulled her hair back gently behind her ears without clipping it.

Thad had returned to the lounge and was reading the paper. She had put the finishing touches to the table and was filling a small bucket with ice when he came out and said, 'Can I do anything to help?'

'You can put the champagne in here, if you like,' she said. 'It's in the fridge.'

He did it without comment, hardly glancing at her as she bent over to peer in the glass door of the oven. The vegetables were all cooked and keeping warm in the roomy drawer at the bottom of the stove, and she had sprinkled a crumbly topping on the casserole and was waiting for it to go the right shade of golden brown. She watched while it did.

She turned out the oven and said. 'How about a sherry for starters, in the lounge?' and took off the apron she had tied about her waist, coming close to him to place it on the bench.

Thad moved away and said, 'Fine,' and stood by the door waiting for her to precede him.

She was waiting for him to say she looked nice, but he didn't. Thad had always noticed her clothes, he was that sort of man, and he had particularly liked this dress.

She sat on the sofa while he poured two glasses of sherry, and when he had handed hers to her she made it plain she expected him to sit beside her. She might have imagined the fractional hesitation before he did. It would have been natural for him to sit close and put his arm around her, and she could have snuggled closer while they had their drinks. Instead, he wedged himself in the corner, with his elbow on the back of the sofa, gazing round the room, not touching her.

She raised her glass to him, and said, 'To your homecoming, Thad—and our future.'

He met her eyes then, but she couldn't read the expression in them, unless it was one of faint cynicism. He raised his glass without speaking, and after a small hesitation she took a sip from hers and watched him follow suit.

'How is your mother?' he asked, breaking the small silence that ensued.

'Quite well. She's getting used to the idea of being without Dad, I think. But it hasn't been easy.'

'I suppose it never is.' His gaze was fixed rather broodingly on the drink that he was gently swirling in the glass held in his strong fingers. 'She must have been glad to have you stay with her.'

'I think she was. I've been spending more time here over the last few weeks, to make the break gradually.'

With Thad still in hospital after her father's death it had seemed sensible to stay there rather than move into her own new home without Thad. The farm was only a few miles away, and both the older woman and the younger one had felt the need of company. The house could have been let, the money helping to pay the mortgage on it, but Vanessa could not bring herself to suggest it, preferring to spend some of her nights there, and keep it aired and tidy and ready for Thad's homecoming.

'She'll miss you.'

'Yes, I think so. But she knew it had to come, and she's glad for our sakes. She said she's already had me at home longer than she expected. They didn't expect to have me back after our wedding, after all. Not many girls return home after the honeymoon,' she smiled.

'Not many new brides end up in hospital at the end of

the honeymoon,' he said. 'I was glad your parents insisted on your going to them when you left the hospital. At least I knew you would be cared for, although I was in no state to see to it myself.'

He looked a bit grim about it, she thought, and she quickly said, 'It wasn't your fault, and if my parents hadn't been able to, your family would care for me. They've been wonderful. I'm always included in their family gatherings. But I missed you.'

The look he gave her was enigmatic. 'You haven't been lonely.'

'That's relative, surely. I've been busy, anyway. And I'm a fulltime worker now, you know.'

'Yes. In the bank.'

He was looking down at his sherry, and stirring uneasily, Vanessa said, 'I was lucky to get the job, Thad. Good jobs are scarce in a small place like this, and until you're well again, completely, we'll need the money.'

'I know,' he said curtly. 'The mortgage on this place. Our budget wasn't planned for my spending several months in hospital.'

He hadn't said much when she had told him about the job, apologising because it meant she would be visiting him less often. She had the feeling that he didn't like it, but felt he would have to accept the position.

'It's a lovely house,' she said. 'Our first home. I would hate to have to let it go. You know, I used to come here and just moon over it, thinking about the time when we could both be here, together. It was rather odd coming back from my honeymoon and going home to my parents again. You and I had only had our honeymoon, and there were times when it was—almost as though we'd never been married at all. Times when I felt that I was still Vanessa Morris, and nothing had happened. Our marriage was just some sort of—mirage. Something unreal.'

'It's real,' Thad said harshly, and Vanessa gulped down some sherry, because the way he looked was almost frightening. When she looked at him again the fleeting expression of barely suppressed savagery was gone, but there still remained a grimness about his mouth.

Softly she said, 'I know. I'm so glad you're home again, Thad.'

He said, 'Are you?' His eyes searched her face intently, hard and questioning. She thought, *he needs reassurance,* astonished, and made to move towards him. But he stood up abruptly, tossing off the remainder of his drink, saying, 'When do we eat? I'm hungry.'

Once she would have joked, saying *'Now, oh lord and master, your wish is my command!'* or something equally silly, and he would have responded in kind. But now she was unsure of his mood and his reactions, so she just finished her drink and said, 'I'll go and see if it's ready.'

There was no need to see—she knew it was, but she needed to escape——

The thought brought her up short, suddenly appalled, at the kitchen door, *Escape*—from Thad! *Of course* she didn't want to escape from him—she loved him! And he loved her—didn't he?

But she was afraid. There was something about him that was different, that was—menacing. Some held-in, barely suppressed violence. *What was the matter with him?* Or with her? Was she merely overwrought and imagining things?

'Stop being ridiculous!' she muttered to herself, and jumped as Thad's voice behind her said, 'What?' She hadn't heard him come out of the lounge.

'Nothing,' she said, throwing a smile haphazardly in his direction. 'I'm talking to myself. It's a habit people get into when they're alone.'

Of course, she had hardly ever been alone, but she had to say something.

'Did I scare you?' he asked, following her into the kitchen. She looked fleetingly into his face and thought, *yes, you scare me—and I don't know why*. Aloud, she said, 'I didn't hear you come into the hall.'

He put the champagne on the table and Vanessa served the meal. Everything was perfectly cooked and delicious—she was a good cook—and Thad complimented her with the suavity of a polite dinner guest, so that somehow the praise chilled rather than thrilled her.

They talked about the hospital, and about her family and his. He said, 'Do they know I'm home?'

'Of course I told them you'd be coming home today. Your parents are expecting us over on Sunday. The whole family will be there.'

'I'm surprised my parents didn't come over today.'

'I invited them, but they said we'd want to be alone for a day or so.'

He didn't reply, and the tension that had eased off began to build again. She felt his silence was an implied denial of any such wish.

Vanessa stood up and began to clear dishes away, saying, 'Why don't you ring your parents? I'm sure they'd like that.'

He said, 'Yes. I'll help you with those later.'

But by the time he left the phone she had finished doing the dishes, and had made coffee for them both to take into the lounge.

'You were quick,' he commented, looking at the tidy kitchen.

'There aren't many dishes with only two of us,' she said.

Thad put on a record and sat apart from her, stretching long legs out in front of him. She had an impulse to go and sit on the carpet in front of his chair and rest her head against him. Perhaps she should, to ease the constraint between them. But the recent hurt was too raw, and she stayed where she was.

When he got up to change the record she took out the cups and rinsed them, and when she came back she hesitated on the threshold of the room, hoping he would make some move of welcome, put out his hand and smile, so that she would go to him and be pulled down in the big chair with him, and he would kiss away her fear and her doubts and her hurt bewilderment.

But he didn't move, just sat with his arms folded in front of him, contemplating the Dégas print that they had bought secondhand and re-framed themselves, so she crossed the room and settled on the sofa again, kicking off her shoes to curl her legs beneath her in her favourite position for listening.

It was a record that she particularly liked, but she found herself, tonight, unable to appreciate it.

Thad got up to go to the cupboard of drinks in the corner and poured himself some whisky.

'Want anything?' he asked, and although she didn't, she asked for a gin and lime, because he would have to bring it over, and then he might sit by her, and this awful widening gap which she could feel between them would be at least physically narrower.

He brought it to her, holding it by the rim so that she

couldn't even brush his fingers in the act of taking it from him, without making it terribly obvious. And before she could pluck up courage to say, *'Darling, please sit by me,'* he had moved back to his chair.

He had helped himself to another drink before she had half finished hers, and when he poured his third, she couldn't help asking, 'Thad, should you be drinking so much? You're only just out of hospital.'

'I'm celebrating the fact,' he said. 'I've already asked you not to fuss. Would *you* like another?'

'No, thank you,' she said. Then with a sudden flash of anger she added, 'If your idea of celebrating is to drink yourself insensible, I think I'll go to bed.'

Thad laughed rather nastily and said, 'It's an idea—drinking myself insensible, I mean. I've never tried it, but perhaps now's the time. Goodnight, my love.'

Vanessa stood up, hesitated, and then left the room.

In the bedroom she stripped and pulled on the nightgown she had put ready for tonight, seething with all kinds of conflicting emotions. She went into the bathroom and washed thoroughly, sluicing cold water on her face to kill the hot stinging of her eyes, and fiercely brushed her teeth.

She left the small lamp on her bedside table burning and got into bed and lay wide awake, thinking with furious disappointment of all that had happened since she had collected Thad from the hospital. She simply didn't understand him.

Wild thoughts flitted through her brain. Surely he wasn't unable to lead a normal married life, as a result of the accident? But she knew that wasn't so. The doctor who had talked to her at length about his injuries, as soon as he was out of danger, had been at pains to assure her of that, in the most tactful but unmistakable terms. Besides, Thad's physical reaction when he had held her this afternoon surely proved there was nothing wrong with him in *that* sense.

Perhaps he was self-conscious about the scars on his body—he had hated her to sit on the right side of the bed in the hospital, where she could see his scarred face. And this afternoon it had been broad daylight. But now it was night—they could turn out the light, if it bothered him...

Surely he knew that she wouldn't mind—she had told him so, in the early days of his recovery, when he had said ruefully, half joking, that the accident had quite spoiled his beauty.

'I don't care,' she had answered him. 'I'll love your scars because you got them saving *me*, and if you were the ugliest man on earth I'd still love you.'

He had a private room, then, and she had leaned over to kiss him and had been gathered close to him as he kissed her back with passion that was almost fierce in its intensity, and whispered, 'I hope they let me out of here soon. I can't stand not being able to make love to you properly.' His fingers slipped inside her blouse and she laughed a little and sighed, because she knew how he felt, and the doctor had just told her it was going to be a long time... and as he kissed her again her hand moved from his hair down the cheek that was covered with a dressing, into the collar of his pyjamas and over his warm skin until the bandages interfered again.

But when he let her go he was pale and there was a fine sheen on his forehead, and she realised that he was weak and very tired, and he needed sleep.

Vanessa stirred in the bed, trying to remember when things had changed. Of course, the other visitors that had come to the hospital had precluded too many such interludes, not to mention the comings and goings of the various hospital personnel. She remembered in particular one day when Thad had been feeling much better; when his leg was out of traction and he had been allowed out of bed that morning for a short time. Three times he had pulled her down beside him on the bed with obvious intent, and three times they had been interrupted by a nurse with urgent need to fill in one of the official charts so necessary to the running of a hospital.

He answered their questions civilly enough and even submitted with fairly good grace to having his temperature and pulse taken by the third nurse, but when she had left the room, he demanded, 'Isn't there a lock on that damned door, for heaven's sake?' And when Vanessa looked and said, 'No, there isn't,' he had looked at her with a smouldering light in his eyes that she knew well, and said, 'Well, come here, anyway. I'm going to kiss you properly if the entire hospital staff decides to invade the room and watch me do it. And this time I won't stop for *anybody*.'

'Oh, no!' Vanessa said firmly. '*You* may be kinky, but *I* prefer making love in private. The next one who comes in will probably be Sister, too, and I don't fancy being thrown out for over-stimulating her patient!'

Thad gave her a deliberately sexy smile, and said, 'Wouldn't you like to over-stimulate me?'

Vanessa gave a breathy laugh. 'Yes. But not here. We—you'll just have to be patient a while longer.'

Soon after that they moved him into a four-bedded room, and since it simply wasn't done to draw the curtains round the beds during visiting hours, there followed long months where nothing more intimate than holding hands and quick kisses of greeting and goodbye was possible. She had blamed the lack of privacy for Thad's seeming coolness, and imagined he was restraining from any hint of passion because the frustration was more than he could bear. And sometimes, when he didn't even return her kiss and seemed disinclined to talk, or was irritable and bad-tempered, she had blamed the effects of the accident, and told herself he was tired and unwell.

She could hear the music faintly from the other room, where Thad was sitting alone, drinking whisky and listening to the record player.

It's all wrong! she thought passionately. And giving herself no time to think, she threw back the sheet and got out of bed. She meant to go right up to him and put her arms about him and ask him what was the matter, but when she stopped in the doorway of the lounge and looked across at him, he was staring into his drink with a look of bitter cynicism on his face that stopped her in her tracks. She had never seen him look like that.

He looked up, and their eyes met across the room, hers filled with shocked puzzlement, and his with—it couldn't be—contempt?

Vanessa said, 'It's late, and you've just come out of hospital, Thad. Don't you think you should come to bed?'

His eyes lowered gradually to the deep-dipping neckline of her nightgown, then wandered down further, lingering on every flimsy fold that barely hid the warm flesh underneath, and Vanessa, who had once been shyly delighted by the frank appreciation he had shown of her body, felt shamed and angry. Because this was different this was—a kind of insult, subtle but unmistakable in its naked, unloving lust.

Then he said, slowly and very clearly, 'I'm sick to death of being told what to do and when to do it. I've had a bellyful of it from nurses, doctors, physiotherapists and the rest. And I'm not going to take it from *you,* is that understood?'

'I just thought'—she whispered—'that you must be tired.'

She had not imagined that hateful, mocking look this afternoon, because it was there again now. And she knew, even before he said the words, that she had just invited a repetition of that humiliation. She stood there in her beautiful nightgown, shrivelling inwardly with shame and a kind of horror, as he said in that same slow, deliberate tone, 'I am not tired. And I am not interested in what you're so—insistent on offering me. Not at the moment. I'll let you know when I require your—services.'

Afterwards, she wondered why she hadn't shrieked at him, *liar, liar, liar*! Why she hadn't yelled and thrown things, and called him some of the names he deserved to be called. Not interested? If she had walked across and touched him he would have ignited like an oil-soaked torch. *She knew it!* He *wanted* her. Badly.

But not lovingly. As she turned and walked numbly back to the bedroom, she thought with wonder. *He doesn't love me any more. He wants me, but without love.* Was that why he wouldn't touch her? Because, like her, he knew that lust without love was ugly and destructive and dangerous?

She climbed shivering into bed and turned out the light as though the darkness would blot out thought, blot out memory.

The record player was still going when she finally went to sleep and her last waking thought was—*He hasn't come, thank God. Thank God he hasn't come!*

CHAPTER THREE

In the morning, Vanessa woke with a faint throb behind her temples and a feeling of depression. Her first thought when she looked at the clock on her bedside table was that it was late, and she had a moment's panic before she realised it was Saturday, and of course she didn't have to work. She had taken the day off yesterday to bring Thad home, and didn't return to work until Monday morning. She would have liked a few more days off to spend with Thad, but as she had only been at the bank for a few months, she would lose pay if she did, and she needed all the money she could earn.

Thad! She sat up suddenly, looking at the empty expanse at the other side of the bed, the unused pillow.

She had dived out of the bed towards the door, when a memory of Thad's face last night when she had confronted him in her flimsy nightwear brought her up short, her face stinging with recollection. Slowly she returned to the room, taking a silky but enveloping dressing gown from the wardrobe, and tied the belt of it tightly about her waist before she opened the bedroom door and crossed the hall to the lounge.

The room was gloomy and smelled stale. There was a faint, persistent scratching sound, and she realised that the record player was still switched on, a disc revolving senselessly on the turntable with the needle running over its smooth centre.

She crossed the room and took the needle off, placing the metal arm carefully on its rest, and switched off the machine. The room was very quiet. She went to the windows and pulled back the curtains with swift movements. The nylon runners made a smooth swishing sound, and the sunlight leapt into the room and struck off the square bottle sitting on the small coffee table near the sofa. Last night the bottle had been half full. Now about a quarter of an inch of liquid remained in the bottom of it. Vanessa looked for the glass and found it lying on its side underneath the table. Thad must have missed when he had tried to put it on the tabletop.

He was lying sprawled on the sofa, his head against a cushion, with the scarred side invisible. He had taken off his tie, and his shirt was half-undone, but he still wore his jacket. He was dead to the world. Well, he had said he intended to drink himself insensible, and apparently that was what he had done.

Filled with a sudden icy rage, Vanessa said loudly, 'Good morning!'

He frowned briefly, then went on sleeping.

She stood looking at him, lying there as though he hadn't a care in the world, the shadow of an overnight growth stubbling his chin. Then she bent and picked up the glass that had fallen on the carpet, looked at it briefly to determine its value, and deliberately dropped it on to the dark tiles of the hearth.

It shattered with a very satisfactory noise, and Thad jumped, swore, opened his eyes and sat up, putting a hand to his head almost immediately. Then he raked back his hair with one hand and glared blearily at her across the small room.

'What the hell was that?' he demanded.

'I dropped a glass,' she said. 'Sorry I woke you up. Actually, I wondered if anything *could*.'

'Is that why you did it?'

She hesitated on the brink of pretending it was an accident, then said, 'Actually, yes.'

He dropped his head into his hands and muttered, 'God, I feel awful!'

She said, 'I'm not surprised. Next time you decide to drink yourself into a stupor, would you mind turning off the record-player first? Apart from wasting power, it's a valuable piece of equipment, and it can't do it any good to be left on all night after a record is finished.'

He moved so that his head rested on the back of the sofa, his arms spread out on either side making the gap left by the unbuttoned shirt gape wider. 'There won't be a next time,' he said.

'Isn't that what they all say?' she asked lightly. The expanse of chest she could see was paler than she had ever seen it, but his skin had a natural olive tint so that it was still faintly golden in colour. She could see the beginning of a scar, a fine slash of purple crossing his skin.

'I need a cup of coffee,' he said.

'Then you can get it yourself!'

'You're not going to be the solicitous little wife and get it for me?'

'You told me you didn't want to be fussed over, remember?'

Thad laughed softly, and said, 'So I did.'

Her eyes were still on that scarcely visible, tantalising mark, and she wrenched them away and turned to pick up the small shovel and brush that hung in front of the fireplace, kneeling to sweep up the pieces of the shattered glass.

He said, 'Be careful you don't cut yourself,' as she put the brush down to pick up some of the larger pieces.

'Who's fussing now?' she retorted. She swept up the last small fragments, replaced the brush on its hook, and stood up with the shovel in her hand. She stepped back and caught the edge of her gown under her foot, staggering backwards.

Thad leaped across to her, grabbing her arm to steady the shovel full of glass, and her waist to stop her from falling.

She didn't fall, except against him, but the glass went flying all across the carpet, small vicious pieces studding it as far as the door.

'Don't move!' said Thad.

She wasn't sure she could have if she tried. His arm was clamped tight about her waist, holding her against his chest, and his fingers were like a warm vice on her wrist.

He said, 'Give me that,' and took the shovel from her hand and reached out to put it on the mantelpiece.

'I'm all right now,' she said, making a feeble effort to loosen his hold on her.

'Don't be ridiculous! You've got bare feet and you've just spread glass over the whole damned room!'

Ironically, she said, '*You* slept in your shoes, of course!'

'Of course,' he agreed cordially, and without warning he swung her up into his arms.

'Oh, *Thad*!' she cried. 'Be——'

'Careful!' he said grimly. 'I know. Shut up!'

She did, and he began to move across the room with her. She heard the faint crunch of glass under his shoes, and linked her hands around his neck. As he crossed the hall she slid one back to his shoulder, and when he put her down, just inside the bedroom doorway, she slipped her hand inside his shirt until it was over the small ridge of the scar on his chest. Deliberately, she moved her fingers down its length, caressingly, and then back to the point where she had started. He seemed to be holding his breath, she couldn't feel him move at all, though his hands were still on her waist, steadying her.

Then he lifted one of them and clamped it hard about her wrist, stopping the soft exploration by pulling her hand roughly away.

'Don't!' he said.

'Why? Was I hurting you?'

'You can't hurt me, Vanessa.'

'Then why don't you want to make love to me?' she asked him bluntly, trying to read in his face the answers that she needed so badly.

She could see nothing that helped, only a kind of wary mockery. Wryly, he said, 'I know it's an old excuse, but the fact is I have a thundering headache. I'll go and make that coffee.'

Blankly, Vanessa looked at herself in the mirror, wondering what was wrong with her. He had evaded the issue, of course, knowing quite well, as she did, that it wasn't *right now* she meant, but the whole period since he had come home.

He had seemed more approachable this morning—even his rejection had been at least less cruel than yesterday's. But it was still a rejection.

She went into the bathroom to wash, and thought, trying to see the funny side, *Maybe I use the wrong brand of soap—or toothpaste*. She and Thad had always been able to laugh together. Supposing she marched into the kitchen right now and asked, '*Do you know something my best friend wouldn't tell me?*'

Maybe he would laugh and pull her into his arms, and explain whatever it was that bothered him, and everything would be as it used to be. And maybe he would turn that frightening look of savage mockery on her again, and crush her again with some brutal answer.

No. She couldn't go on like this, trying to invite his love, only to have her advances thrown back in her face. Three times was too much. The next move would have to come from Thad, she decided. Pride and love didn't go together, she had always believed, but a woman could stand only so much; constant humiliation wasn't part of the deal.

She made the bed and dressed in jeans and a cotton knit top before going to the kitchen. Thad was sitting at the table, drinking a cup of black coffee.

Vanessa took a bowl of eggs and some bacon out of the refrigerator and asked him politely, 'Are you hungry?'

'No, thanks,' he mumbled, and reached for more coffee. When she had cooked hers and sat down at the table with it, he looked across, shuddered, and stumbled to his feet. 'I'll have a shower,' he said, and went out of the room.

Vanessa almost laughed. It was his own fault, she reflected, with a certain satisfaction, if he felt so awful. Serve him right!

Showered and shaved, he looked considerably better, but she stopped herself from asking him how he felt. After doing the dishes she swept up the glass again and got out the vacuum cleaner, smiling sweetly at him when he gave her a martyred look at the sound of its busy whine and took himself off outside to get away from it.

When she had finished the vacuuming she did the dusting and cleaned out the bathroom. Thad had hung his towel tidily and left everything neat. She had his mother to thank for that. With a family of four boys and one girl, she had trained them all well, and Thad had learned early to tidy up after himself.

The family would be expecting them tomorrow. She hoped that Thad would not be so bearish with *them*.

She managed to keep herself busy all morning, pushing to the back of her mind the knowledge that this wasn't at all what she had planned for Thad's first full day at home, and she cooked a more elaborate lunch than she had intended, making a finicky salad with a garnish of rosette tomatoes and finely grated cheese that took ages to prepare.

Thad seemed to have regained his appetite, making a hearty meal of the salad, the small buttered potatoes and the grilled lamb chops, and eating four of the fruit muffins she had baked and served straight from the oven.

'You're a wonderful cook, Vanessa,' he complimented her.

'Is that why you married me?' she asked lightly.

He flashed her a penetrating look before he answered, 'Yes, of course.'

It should have gone on from there, bantering and teasing until he swooped on her or she fell into his arms, but she dried up, suddenly, afraid it wouldn't be like that, afraid of getting hurt again. And Thad didn't pursue the subject, either.

When they had finished he helped her with the dishes and she said, 'What would you like to do this afternoon?'

'Laze around in that sunshine out there,' he replied.

'Might as well take advantage of the good weather while it lasts.'

'I might join you,' she said. 'I haven't had much chance to acquire a tan this summer.'

His eldest brother had given them a couple of lounging chairs when they got married, and she reminded him that they were stowed in the small garden shed behind the house, before she went off to get changed.

She put on a brief bikini of red satin with white cotton cords tying round the neck and at the sides of the pants, and took a pair of sunglasses and a book before she strolled out to the back garden. He had pulled out the two chairs and placed one in the dappled shade of a wattle tree, the other a few feet away in full sun. He was already stretched out on the one under the tree, hands behind his head, and eyes closed. He hadn't changed from the grey slacks and patterned shirt he had put on after his shower that morning.

Vanessa settled herself on the chair without speaking, put on the sunglasses and opened her book.

After about half an hour, Thad hadn't moved, and she had read two pages of her book. She took off her sunglasses, looked at him, and sighed. Disconcertingly, he opened his eyes and looked straight at her.

'Something the matter?' he asked.

Yes—but his tone was cold and she didn't dare say it.

She shook her head and closed her book.

'Isn't the book interesting?' he asked.

'Not particularly,' she answered, wondering if she was imagining that his question had a forced air, as though he was making conversation.

She got up and pulled the thin mattress from the chair

on to the ground, and stretched herself out on it, face down.

Thad asked, 'Have you used suntan lotion?'

'No. I forgot.'

'You have got some, haven't you?'

'In the bathroom cupboard, but I'm too lazy to get it.'

After a few moments she heard his chair give a faint squeak, and looked up to see him making towards the house. She wondered if he would change into something cooler, but when he emerged from the house a little later he was still fully dressed.

He came over to her and put the bottle of suntan lotion down beside her. Then he went back to his chair and when she didn't move said curtly, 'Put the stuff on.'

Reluctantly she sat up and smeared some of the lotion on her shoulders, arms and legs. Then, smiling to herself a little, she lay down on her stomach again and unhooked the fastening at the back of her bikini top.

'Do my back for me, please, Thad,' she said casually.

She didn't dare look at him, almost holding her breath. Then his chair squeaked again, and a few moments later she felt a cold blob of moisture land on her back. She gasped and wriggled upwards, but his hand slapped firmly down on her back and he began spreading the lotion over it with long, firm strokes.

She settled back on to the mattress and closed her eyes. His hand was shiveringly familiar, following the contours of her back, moving from the curve of her waist to her shoulder blades, and down to where the bikini pants started. It wakened sensations that made her breath quicken, and started a train of thought that made her cheeks go warm. She wanted Thad to go on for ever with this delicious stroking, it was so smooth, so warm, so sensationally sensuous.

Then the stroking stopped, and for a moment or two his hand rested where it was, just below the small of her back—and then it was gone.

She lay holding her breath, wondering what would happen if she turned over on to her back, what expression she would see on his face, how he would react if she smiled at him and held up her arms ...

Then his clipped voice said, 'That should be enough. Remember it's dangerous to sunbathe without some sort of protection.'

The bottle, re-capped, landed just within her vision on the grass, and she heard his chair accepting his weight again as he went back to it.

Vanessa lay like a stone, bereft of all feeling, all emotion. She could only be, in a remote way, glad that she had not invited another rejection.

A long time later, she fumbled behind her to do up the strap of her bra, and then sat up. Thad was watching her, his face unreadable.

Choosing her words carefully, she said, 'Don't you want to get a tan, too?'

'All in good time,' he said calmly. 'I've enough of a head already without sitting out in that blazing sun.'

'Is it still aching?'

'Still.'

'Have you taken something for it? There's aspirin in the bathroom ...'

'I'll be all right. I've had so many drugs in the hospital I've vowed never to take another pill unless I'm in desperate need. I'll survive. Besides, it's no doubt a well-deserved penance.'

Vanessa shot a glance at him. 'For what?'

There was a tiny silence before he said, 'For over-indulgence. Isn't there something about the sin finding out the sinner—words to that effect?' He looked, fleetingly, as he had once or twice before, when he had become a frightening stranger to her.

Quickly she said, 'I don't know what that means. Do you?'

His mouth moved into an oddly bitter curve, momentarily, and he said, 'Not really. Perhaps I'm in the process of finding out.'

They went inside when it began to get cool, and Vanessa cooked a quick meal which they ate early.

When the dishes were done, she asked, 'Are you tired?'

'Not particularly. Why?'

'I thought it might be nice to go for a walk.'

'All right.'

'We won't go far,' she said. 'Just down to the river and back.'

'In deference to my semi-invalid state?'

'I'm trying not to fuss,' she explained. 'But they did tell me to look after you, and not to let you do too much at first.'

'You're very conscientious.'

'I'm your wife,' she said quietly. 'That's what being married is all about, isn't it? Caring for each other. *You* made me put on that suntan lotion this afternoon.'

Thad inclined his head slightly ironically, as though conceding the point to her, and didn't answer.

It was peaceful by the river, quiet and soothing. It was not a particularly pretty river, for like many North Island rivers its water tended to be muddy and sluggish as it neared the sea some ten miles away. But at this point there was an old wooden bridge from which the local children, and sometimes their parents, fished or set eel-traps, and the banks were lined with weeping willows that drooped gracefully into the lapping water. A few ducks floated on its surface near the brown-tipped raupo bullrushes on the far bank, and a brilliant royal-blue pukeko on his long scarlet legs stalked along with dignified unconcern among tufts of marshy grass just up from the river. A vee-shaped flight of black swans passed overhead, and they watched them until they were out of sight in the pale evening sky, with its glimmering stars just beginning to appear.

Thad leaned beside her on the railing of the old bridge, and she wished he would take her hand or put a companionable arm about her, but he didn't. And after a while he straightened up and said, 'Had enough?' as though he was anxious to go.

As they retraced their steps past the dairy factory with its huge stainless steel milk silos outside, and the tankers neatly parked in formation beside it, Vanessa dared to slip a hand into his arm, and, feeling him stiffen at her touch, rather wished that she hadn't.

Among the modest wooden bungalows in their quarter-acre sections lining the road, was one belonging to Vanessa's sister and her husband. Just as they were passing, Vanessa's brother-in-law opened the front door and stepped out on to the path, holding some milk bottles.

'Thad!' he shouted in delight, bringing Beth out of the house to see them, too, followed by two of their three small children.

Vanessa was reluctant to accept their invitation to come inside, but while she was formulating excuses, Thad had already accepted, and was holding open the wooden gate.

Vanessa was very fond of Beth and Mitch, and had always enjoyed her small niece and two nephews, but she had hoped that she and Thad were a little closer today, a little more 'normal' than they had been yesterday, and had been looking forward to a quiet evening together. She murmured something to Beth about only staying a little while, since Thad mustn't overtire himself, and as she turned to find a chair found him looking at her satirically, as though he had overheard.

Perhaps as a sort of punishment, he deliberately ignored all her attempts to leave after an hour or so, apparently enjoying himself immensely talking to Mitch and Beth.

When they finally left it was quite late, and Vanessa felt taut and strained and unhappy, sure that Thad was deliberately putting off the time when they would be alone again together.

They walked home through the dark in silence broken only by the persistent song of invisible crickets and the occasional roar of a passing car. As they neared their house another car passed, and on the other side of the road they caught a glimpse of a transfixed opossum, huge eyes shining golden orange in the headlights, and bushy tail erect.

Vanessa stopped. 'The silly thing will get run over if he goes on the road,' she said. 'Can you see him?'

Thad stepped to the edge of the footpath and waved his arms, and the small cat-like shape loped away into the darkness.

Vanessa laughed and said, 'If anyone saw you, they'd think you were mad!'

'Perhaps I am,' he said in the darkness, and turned to walk on.

As soon as they got into the house, tension seemed to

lap about them in waves, like something tangible and inescapable.

'Are you tired?' she asked, simply for words to break the silence.

'Not particularly—are you?'

She evaded that. 'I napped this afternoon, in the sun,' she lied. She hadn't dozed at all, but lain there for ages, tensely wondering if *he* was asleep, or if he was secretly watching her ...

She offered him a cup of coffee, but he said, 'I've had enough coffee at Beth's, thanks.' His face was taut and his black eyes avoided hers.

He went into the lounge and switched on the television. Vanessa followed him, and saw that the programme was an ancient western, with a peculiarly smooth-skinned young James Stewart looking oddly akin to the white horse that he was riding.

'Are you going to watch that?' she asked from the doorway, watching Thad settle into an armchair.

'I like Westerns,' he said mildly. 'But if you prefer the other channel——'

'No.' She didn't even know what was on the other channel, and certainly had no desire to watch it. 'I'm going to bed,' she said abruptly.

He said, 'Goodnight,' and returned his attention to the flickering black-and-white images on the screen.

For a moment Vanessa stood there, then she turned and went into the bedroom. She undressed slowly and prepared for bed, trying to make her mind a blank, tired of the endless wondering and speculation. She took a book and propped herself against the pillows and tried to read. Some time later the muted sound from the television stopped, and she held her breath, wondering if Thad would come to bed.

He didn't, and with a kind of stubbornness she sat on, holding the book and not taking in more than a third of what she was reading.

After half an hour she angrily threw down the book and switched off the light. Let him spend another uncomfortable night on the sofa if he wanted to, she certainly wasn't going to go and ask him again to come to bed. She was thoroughly fed up with his unfathomable moods.

When he did come in, some time later, she was still awake, lying with closed eyes waiting vainly for sleep to come. She heard him take out his pyjamas and go to the bathroom, and the soft hiss of the shower that followed.

When he came softly back into the room she knew he was standing by his side of the bed, and suddenly thinking, *Why should I pretend to be asleep?* she opened her eyes and looked at his shadowy outline in the darkness.

'You're awake,' he said.

'Yes, I was waiting for you.'

He hesitated a moment longer before he got into bed and lay back on the pillow, with one hand up behind his head. She could see he was staring up into the darkness.

'I couldn't sleep until you came,' she said softly.

Slowly he turned his head, and said, 'I'm here now. Go to sleep.'

Incredibly, the tension oozed away in the darkness, and some kind of peace seemed to settle in her soul. She felt suddenly overwhelmingly tired, and her eyes closed of their own accord as she drifted into sleep.

CHAPTER FOUR

VANESSA was glad they had arranged to go to Thad's parents' farm the next day. It would be a large, noisy gathering and perhaps that was what they both needed, to get things into perspective.

She rolled her bikini in a towel and pushed it into a casual bag after she had dressed, and as Thad came in after using the bathroom, she said, 'Shall I put your togs in here with mine?'

He looked up from buttoning his shirt and asked, 'Are we swimming?'

'Your parents installed a pool while you were in the hospital—don't you remember me telling you about it?'

He tucked in his shirt and said, 'Several people told me about it, actually. But yes, it had slipped my mind.'

'Well——?'

His eyes met hers briefly across the room, indifferently. 'Please yourself,' he said, shrugging his shoulders.

Vanessa opened a drawer and rummaged for the brief maroon shorts he had worn for swimming on their honeymoon. 'It doesn't commit you to going in,' she said tightly. Some simmering resentment made her add, as she turned to drop the briefs into her bag, 'You needn't even put them on if you're scared to . . .'

'*Scared?*' His voice was harsh with anger.

She stayed staring down at the bag, but his hand clamped hard on her upper arm and he pulled her round roughly to face him.

'What the hell are you talking about?' he demanded.

'Never mind,' she said defeatedly, trying to turn away.

His other hand caught at her other arm, stopping her. She made a sharp, protesting movement, and he jerked her closer, his fingers digging into her flesh until they hurt. '*What* do you mean—scared?' he demanded.

The pain of his grip made her angry. 'What I said!' she almost shouted at him. 'If you're afraid of people seeing your scars, you don't need to swim, that's all!'

His mouth looked hard and angry, and his face seemed to have become paler. Suddenly sorry, sure she should have been more understanding and compassionate, she said more softly, with a note of desperation, 'Oh, *Thad*! You needn't be self-conscious! You're not ugly, believe me—certainly not to me—or to your family, I'm sure. And does anyone else matter, really? Shall I tell you what I was thinking on Friday, at the hospital, when you locked me out while you were dressing? I was thinking, I'd like to kiss every scar you got saving me. I'll never forget you throwing yourself across me in the car, and I thought we'd both be killed ... Darling, why be ashamed of—of marks of courage and unselfishness?'

His expression hadn't altered, except to grow subtly more enigmatic.

'Is that what you think?' he said at last. 'That I'm worried about my looks—hiding myself away behind clothes because of a few marks on my skin? What exactly do you think I am? Narcissus?'

He let her go suddenly, but stood looking down at her accusingly.

'Then——' she said, softly challenging, 'if you're not bothered by them, why have you been so—so cold with me?'

'You mean, why don't I make love to you?' he said flatly. 'Perhaps because I no longer find you attractive—maybe two weeks was enough. You're beautiful—but there are lots of beautiful girls.'

Vanessa felt as though she must have swayed with the cruelty of it. But she lifted her chin defiantly at him, and said steadily, 'That is ridiculous and untrue. I don't know why you should say it, why you want to hurt me. But I *know* I could make you take it back, like *that*!' She snapped her fingers.

His eyes were filled with cold violence, and they went over her mercilessly from her face to her feet and back again, so that if the bed had not been behind her knees she would have stepped back in an instinctive effort to escape their scrutiny.

'I wouldn't,' he warned softly. 'You might get a whole lot more than you bargained for!' Then he turned away from her, and said curtly, 'We're expected, aren't we? Let's go.'

They were seated next to each other at lunch, but they never addressed a word to each other. Not that anyone seemed to notice. Thad's family could easily have been a bit overwhelming for outsiders. Thad's parents were both tall people, and their four sons took after them. Bret was the eldest, and Ken came next. The two of them were in partnership in a mobile machinery business. Bret's wife, Clementina, was a tall, elegant redhead he had brought back from England with him last year, and who was now running a successful boutique business in Auckland using her own designs. Ken's wife, Elaine, was a quiet, pretty girl who was kept busy looking after a lively two-year-old daughter and a new baby. The other Nelson son, Carl, was at present overseas, teaching in British Columbia. And the only girl, Nicola, a small, lively brunette, had married Owen Page, a big man as tall as her brothers—in the hope, she said, that he would protect her from them. Their baby boy sat happily gurgling around a rusk biscuit while lunch went on.

There was plenty of lively chatter around the big family table to distract attention from the strained atmosphere between Thad and his wife, and no one seemed to notice anything amiss.

Vanessa volunteered to help with the dishes afterwards, relieved to escape to the kitchen for a while. When they had finished, she stayed in the kitchen for a while chatting to Clem and Nicola and admiring the baby.

Then Bret came in, dressed for swimming, and asked them if they were going to sit there all day or come into the pool with the rest of the family. He teased his wife, and as Clem put her hand into his outstretched one and rose to go with him, Vanessa watched them wistfully, as she saw the way they looked at each other. In the doorway, Bret turned and met her eyes and raised his eyebrows a fraction.

She wondered if he had read her mind. She and Bret had once had a special sort of relationship, and she had always felt closer to him than to the other members of Thad's family, although she liked them all. She got her bag and as she removed her swimsuit and towel, realised that Thad must have taken his while she was drying the dishes.

When she and Nicola, carrying the baby dressed in an absurd scrap of red stretch nylon, emerged from the house and walked over to the pool, it was impossible to distinguish Thad's dark head from the others in the water, at first. There was a splashy game of water-polo going on with a colourful beach ball, and for a while the two girls sat on towels at the poolside with the baby. Then the game petered out and Nicola slid in, holding her son in her arms, introducing him gently to the water, and Vanessa too slipped into the water for a leisurely swim of the length. Thad and Bret were still in, but Thad ignored her.

She stayed in for about half an hour, and other people got in and out in varying combinations, but Thad was still in the water.

Vanessa got out and wrung out her hair and went to sit on a towel to comb it out. She had nearly finished when a movement at the poolside caught her eye and she saw Thad pulling himself out, pushing his dripping hair out of his eyes as he stood up. The comb stilled as she caught her breath, watching the lithe play of muscle under his taut olive skin, with the water dripping over its smooth surface, matting the fine hairs on his chest and legs, and whitening the scars on his body.

And then he threw back his head and saw her looking at him, and his eyes were cold and hard and calculating.

Hot tears filled her own eyes, and she didn't know if it was for the pain he had suffered that those whitened scars symbolised, or the pain he had inflicted on her with his suggestion that he no longer loved her.

She threw down the comb and turned over on her stomach on to the towel, burying her face in her folded arms to hide the tears. Then she stiffened as a towel landed softly beside hers, very close, and she knew that Thad had lowered his body to lie beside her, almost, but not quite, touching her.

Against the babble of sound all about them, he said, 'What are you crying for?'

'I'm not,' she said.

His arm touched the back of her head as hard fingers curled on to her cheek and felt the moisture there. She moved convulsively and his hand encircled her arm, his arm suddenly hard across her back, pinning her where she was. Close to her other ear, his implacable voice murmured, 'Why are you crying?'

Vanessa refused to answer, clenching her teeth to stop the tears from welling up again.

Thad said, 'Look at me.'

'No. Let go my arm,' she said. 'You're hurting me.'

'I *said*, look at me!' he repeated. And he did, momentarily, let her arm go, only to shift his grip and pull her over on to her back.

Vanessa gave a soft, outraged shriek and hit out at him, but he caught her flailing arm before she could do any damage.

Furiously, she whispered, 'Do you think you can manhandle me in front of your entire family? I've only to yell——'

'They'll think you're fooling,' he said, his mouth smiling while his eyes remained cold and watchful, examining the smudged remains of the tears still on her face. 'There's a lot of it about.'

Wildly, she glanced around, and saw what he meant. Nicola was struggling in a purposeful Bret's arms and calling plaintively for her husband's help, but Owen pretended to be engrossed in playing with his small son. Little Sara was shrieking too—with delight, as Ken bounced her up and down in the cool water of the pool, and even Clem and Elaine had been drawn into a laughing, protesting game of splash with Mr Nelson. Mrs Nelson was lying in a deckchair some distance away, with a magazine over her face.

A loud splash brought Vanessa's attention back to the pool. Bret was standing by the side, dusting his hands, and she said confidently, '*Bret* won't!' and drew in a breath to call him.

But she never did it, because Thad simply moved a little and swiftly covered her parted lips with his, in a hard, merciless kiss. And when he lifted his head a little, from the corner of her eye she saw Bret sauntering in the other direction.

And Thad's face had changed, and when he bent his head to hers again, his mouth had changed as well. No longer angry and punishing, it was soft and seeking instead, so that she shivered and then responded, her taut resistance to his hold melting away in a lovely, tingling wave of passion. His hand moved and began caressing her, and she caught at it and moved her head in protest, murmuring against his mouth, 'Thad! Everyone can see!'

'Let them,' he said lazily. But he moved a little away, still holding her, his lips against her earlobe. 'Now tell me why you cried.'

Was that why he had kissed her so gently, so coaxingly? Because force hadn't worked, and persuasion might do instead? A slow, soft anger stirred in her. Only hours ago he had said he didn't want to make love to her. Now, having changed his mind, apparently, he took *her* reciprocation for granted. And having got from her the answer to his question, would he spurn her again? He couldn't have his cake and eat it too—she wasn't going to be a victim of his cruel and inexplicable games. The stirring anger became sharp and violent, and she pushed hard and suddenly at his shoulders and said, 'Go to hell!' as he rolled away with the suddenness of her attack. Then she was free and running to the pool to dive into its clean depths and wash away the feel of his mouth, his hands.

When his lean body scythed into the water beside her, she turned to streak away, but he caught her leg, and when she kicked out at him, pulled her under until she stopped, and then got his arms about her waist as they both surfaced.

She struggled fiercely until they both went under again, limbs entwined in the cool silent world of the pool. When she stopped fighting he took them both to the surface again, and his arms held her while they floated together, gasping in air. There was a hard, sensual recklessness in his face that matched the reluctant, stirring excitement in her.

Trying to fight it, she demanded, 'Do you want to drown me?'

'Maybe,' Thad said tersely, and holding on to the bar at the side of the pool with one hand, he hauled her close with the other and kissed her with a kind of controlled savagery, so that she protested with a little sound in her throat, and pushed against his chest in an effort to avoid it.

Bret's voice said tolerantly, 'Hey, break it up, you two. You've been called twice already.'

Thad eased his grip on Vanessa, and she looked up into Bret's face where he was crouching by the edge of the pool, holding two tall glasses. She saw the quick, puzzled frown in his eyes before he said casually, 'Do you want them there, or are you coming out?'

'I'm coming out,' Vanessa said quickly, and put up a hand for him to help her.

He put down the drinks and took her hands in his, and as she was hoisted upwards Vanessa felt Thad's hands slide down the length of her, caressingly down from her waist to her hips and thighs as she left him. Then they were all three standing at the poolside, and Bret had handed her a drink as they strolled towards the others.

She stayed with the group from then on, and made sure she was not alone with Thad for the rest of the day.

Towards the end of the afternoon, when Nicola and Owen had gone, and Elaine and Ken were saying goodbye, Bret drew her aside. She had been aware once or twice of him looking at her thoughtfully, and she thought he was watching Thad too. So she wasn't really surprised when he steered her around the corner of the house to a quiet corner of the verandah, where he pushed her on to the broad rail in the corner so that she could lean on the end of the house, and stood with his hand against the corner post himself.

Quietly, he asked, 'What's going on, then, Vanessa?'

It wouldn't do to deny there was anything wrong. Bret knew her too well. And she supposed he knew his younger brother even better.

Helplessly, she spread her hands and said, 'I wish I knew, Bret.'

'Can you tell me about it?'

She bit her lip, thinking. But there was so much she couldn't say, even to Bret. So much that was intensely personal and private, so much that hurt ...

'That was no ordinary kiss I interrupted this afternoon,' Bret said quietly. 'Thad looked savage, and you looked shattered.'

'Was it so obvious?'

'Yes. Look—I don't want to interfere in your marriage, Vanessa. But I'm damned fond of you both, and Thad *has* just come out of hospital. That should mean the two of you ought to be happy as a pair of turtle-doves, but it's been a long hard strain on your relationship. It probably isn't really surprising if things are a bit rocky for a while. Most couples would find it difficult to adjust after such a long separation. You and Thad didn't even have time to get your marriage on its feet before it was taking shocks that would have wrecked many a marriage.'

'Yes, but—Bret, do you think Thad might regret having married at all? I know very well he could have had practically any girl he wanted, for the asking. I mean, he *was* a bit of a——'

'A bit of a lad with the girls? Sure—he knocked 'em dead. All except you and Clementina—who treated him like a brother from the first, much to his surprise.' Bret grinned. 'And you just refused to be impressed, which did him a power of good. So he had to have you.'

'Yes. And now he doesn't want me.'

For a moment Bret said nothing. Then: 'I'm sure that isn't true.'

'I can't believe it either. But it's what he said.'

'Why, the stupid young——!' He moved to touch her shoulder. 'You didn't take him seriously, did you? Thad always had a pretty fierce temper, you know. I'd advise you not to take much notice of what he says in anger.'

'It's not quite that simple,' she said. Then, thinking it out, she went on, 'Bret, there might have been another reason Thad wanted me—had to have me, as you said.'

'I phrased it badly,' Bret said swiftly. 'He was frankly head over heels in love with you, Vanessa. You must know that.'

'Perhaps,' she said. 'But he also thought of me as once having been *your* girl.'

'Surely you told him——'

'I tried to, but he didn't want to hear. Bret, I know how

close this family is, but you are the eldest, and dominant. I've sometimes thought there's an element of rivalry in Thad's feeling for you.'

Bret lifted an amused eyebrow. 'That sounds very Freudian. Are you suggesting he's jealous?'

'Not exactly, but all his life he's competed with you, in a way—he isn't the sort of man who likes being second, even to his brother. Maybe—marrying me, he was trying to prove something to himself.'

'For heaven's sake, Vanessa. He's thirty now, not thirteen!'

'He was still jealous of my relationship with you, right up until we got married—even after you married Clem. I did want him to understand how it was, with us, but he simply refused to let me speak of it at all. He said he didn't want to know anything about my past, and he wasn't going to tell me anything about his—except what we couldn't help knowing about each other ...'

'Then,' Bret said slowly, 'does that mean he doesn't know about Ross?'

Vanessa looked down at her hands. 'He knows there was someone,' she said. 'He doesn't know who. He said he didn't care.'

'Meaning he didn't want to know. That's just as well, I guess, in the circumstances ..' Bret paused, then abruptly asked, 'Why did you take that job at the bank?'

'It was offered, and I needed the money ...'

'I *told* you——'

'I know, I know. You would have been glad to help. Thad didn't want to accept it.' She saw the quick contraction of Bret's mouth and eyebrows and said, 'He wouldn't even take help from your parents, Bret. He's proud.'

'I know *that*!' Bret said grimly. 'How does he feel about you working?'

'It's normal these days. He does feel bad about not being able to work himself, though, I think.'

'How *is* your job?' Bret asked. 'No strings?'

Vanessa smiled faintly, and coloured. 'No strings—I made sure of that before I accepted. Ross has changed, Bret. After all, our affair was over nearly six years ago.'

'After which he spread unsavoury tales about you all over the district.'

'He did apologise for that, when he offered me the job. He said some unkind things once, to someone he trusted, and he hadn't intended it to go any further. And he hoped I'd take the job as a sort of reparation. At least, that's what he implied.'

'And he hasn't made a pass at you since you began working for him?'

Vanessa looked away, her cheeks burning.

'Vanessa!' Bret put his hands on her shoulders and pulled her up on to her feet facing him. 'He *has*, hasn't he?'

'It was nothing, Bret—honestly! It was after the Christmas party at the bank—he took me home.'

'*Why*, for God's sake?'

'Because it was late, and dark, and he passes my house anyway! Why not?'

'All right, I'm sorry.' He took his hands away, but still stood in front of her. 'What happened?' he asked, with resignation.

'*Nothing!* He'd had a bit to drink, and knew it. He asked if I'd make him some coffee, and as he was driving I thought it was a good idea, and invited him in.' Bret momentarily closed his eyes, then wryly opened them again.

'He made a pass, and I said no, and he left. The next day he apologised, and said it would never happen again. And it hasn't.'

'And you're sure it won't.'

'Quite sure.'

'You always did have far too much faith in human nature, my girl. Didn't it occur to you what a risk you were taking?'

'I'm a big girl now, Bret. I *have* dealt with amorous drunks before. And he wasn't even very drunk—just a bit high. As manager of the bank, he can't afford to——'

'Drunk or not, he's a man and much stronger than you. What if he hadn't taken no for an answer?'

'Men usually do, if you mean it—and haven't given them any encouragement beforehand. Besides, I don't think rape would do his reputation much good with the bank, either. He's very ambitious, you know.'

From the corner of her eye Vanessa caught a movement at the other end of the verandah. She turned her head, and Bret did the same thing, and Thad was standing there, watching them.

Just for an instant she had the impression that he was somehow coiled and waiting, like a tiger about to spring. Then he moved, and walked towards them, and smiled. But the smile missed his eyes, that were black and dangerous.

'Secrets?' he asked lightly.

'No, of course not,' Bret said easily, putting a companionable arm around Vanessa's shoulders, perhaps because he sensed she needed his support.

Because she was aware that she wouldn't have liked Thad to overhear the conversation, Vanessa felt she looked guilty, and Thad, glancing from her face to Bret's, stood, feet apart, looking vaguely belligerent, although his mouth still wore the imitation smile. Bret's arm dropped as they drew near him, and he gave her a tiny push towards her husband.

'Looking for your wife?' he enquired, as though nothing in the world could possibly be the matter. 'I guess I'd better find Clementina, too. It's time we made tracks. We have further to go than you two.'

'We've been asked to stay on for tea,' Thad said to Vanessa. 'Mother said it would save you cooking when we get home, and there's plenty left from lunch.'

'Oh, that would be nice!' said Vanessa, relieved at anything so normal and ordinary, and thinking that he probably preferred to stay, too. 'I'll—go and see if I can help,' she added, suppressing an instinct to sidle past him. She met his eyes briefly as she stepped round him, because he wasn't moving, and they seemed to her to be both wary and accusing; his face still had that waiting look, as though he was an enemy, biding his time.

CHAPTER FIVE

MILKING had to be done before they could eat, and as the farm worker Mr Nelson employed had the weekend off, Thad helped in the cowshed. Guiltily, Vanessa felt his temporary absence as a welcome respite.

Thad's mother didn't seem to find anything wrong, and talked quite happily to Vanessa as they prepared the meal and waited for the men to come in.

When they did, the tension began again. Thad spoke easily and even at times jokingly with his parents, but only addressed a remark to Vanessa when he had to, and the flicker of his eyes on her was a brief searing every time he looked her way, holding a kind of cold flame that frightened her.

They sat on the front verandah afterwards, until the creeping shadows of the night descended from the distant bush-covered hills and crept across the green paspallum grass of the paddocks; until the spiky cabbage trees by the gate were no longer etched against a violent sky and had been swallowed up in darkness. The birds that gathered every evening in the big totara tree next to the house gradually twittered into sleepy silence, and their shrill chorus was replaced by the soprano throbbing of a thousand crickets. The night was warm and humid and Vanessa, listening with a very careful appearance of casual interest to the talk about her, gently eased her skirt away from her legs, moving its soft folds a little because it felt as though the fabric was sticking to her body.

Thad was sitting on the top step, his back against the supporting post of the verandah, while the other three had chairs. He had been talking to his father, his face in profile to her, but at her movement he turned his head quickly and asked, 'What is it? You want to go?'

'Nothing,' she said. 'It's hot.'

She didn't know if she wanted to go home. They had to go some time, but she was frankly nervous of him.

Thad suddenly said, 'Come for another swim.' He turned to his mother and father for permission and they both endorsed the idea.

'Count us out, though,' said his mother, smiling. 'I'm going in.

Mr Nelson rose too, echoing her, and Thad stood up and held out his hand to Vanessa.

She said, 'It's late, Thad. I'm not sure that I——'

His hand descended on her wrist, pulling her on to her feet. Smiling, he said, 'We're going swimming in the moonlight, Vanessa. Get your things.'

When she had changed he was waiting, still dressed, on the verandah.

'Come on, then.' He held her wrist again, his eyes dark with challenge.

He kept his hold on her as though not trusting her to follow, and they walked through the gentle darkness to the pool. A row of trees separated the pool area from the house, and the inky blackness was broken only by the rippling of fitful moonlight on the water of the pool, and the lightness of the concrete surround.

'Aren't you going to change?' she asked.

'Yes, I left my towel and togs here this afternoon,' he said, and turned away into the darkness for a few moments, coming back with them in his hand. He dropped them on the grass and began unbuttoning his shirt.

Hastily Vanessa dropped her towel beside his and went to the edge of the pool and slipped quickly into the water. The first shock was cold, but the sun had been on it all day, and soon it began to feel warm and soothing. She swam to the end and then turned on her back, just in time to see Thad poised at the other end before he dived in. The darkness was less impenetrable now, with a pale moon frosting the tips of the waves she had made, and she could see the blurred outline of his body, with no dark strip about his hips. He hadn't bothered to put on his shorts.

When he surfaced beside her she turned over and began a fast crawl for the far end of the pool. He paced her, and when she turned and started back again, he came too, and in the last two yards streaked ahead and was waiting for her when she reached the end, reaching out his arms to scoop her into them. Their bodies were smooth and cool with the water, and his eyes were fathomless, nothing but a gleam in the darkness. Vanessa sensed an elemental excitement in him—it was redolent in his hands on her bare wet skin, the white glimpse of a tight smile, the taut muscularity of his arms about her waist and back, his thighs against hers.

She had swum faster than her usual pace, and her breath came quickly. She threw back her head, trying to see his features, his expression, but it was too dark and shadowed. He dipped his head and his cool lips found hers—not gently at all. The coolness vanished in a hunting, hurting kiss that seemed to express an angry desire to bruise her into some sort of submission.

Frightened and furious, she kicked against him, but the water impeded her. Pushing against him with her hands was futile, and she couldn't free her arms enough to hit at him.

At last he lifted his head, and his hold slackened a little, and she lashed out, freeing herself and thumping a fist against his hard chest, digging her nails into the arms that encircled her, raking at his face. His arms fell away and she dived away from him, trying to swim diagonally to the side so that she could get out.

She was almost there, and just out of her depth, when Thad caught her, his hands slipping along her wet limbs as she silently fought him, the water splashing about them while they struggled, she for freedom, and he for mastery. But she was handicapped by his greater strength and the depth of the water. He could stand with his feet on the bottom of the pool. She stopped struggling when he finally got both her hands firmly gripped in one of his, behind her back, and the other hand was holding her by the hair. She felt the tug of her hair, moving her head backwards down to the water so that it lapped at the tips of her earlobes, and she automatically gasped in a breath as panic filled her, and a fantastic idea that he was actually going to drown her.

Then his lips were on the wet skin of her throat, skimming slowly along the length of it in a sensuous caress, and she lay helplessly floating while he explored the smooth taut line of it again and again. Then he moved again, releasing her hands, and his body was suddenly beneath hers, both of them on their backs and floating in the water, and his hands were on her waist and on her breast as he kicked gently to carry them to the end of the pool. Languidly Vanessa relaxed against him.

'Get out,' he said softly.

She climbed out and walked with shaking legs to the light blur on the dark grass where their towels were. She picked one up, and pressed it over her face and rubbed briefly at her hair, before Thad's hand from behind plucked it away. She made a protesting sound that turned to a gasp as his hands pulled her back against him, his fingers hard against her stomach, curving about her ribcage. His mouth was on her shoulder, warm and exploratory.

She trembled, and said, 'We'd better go home.'

'No.'

He might as well have slapped her. By all the signs, he surely wanted to make love to her.

In a fury of exasperation, she made a violent movement of her shoulder, so that he jerked up his head. 'What the hell do you *want*?' she cried.

'Don't be bloody silly!' he said roughly. He turned her suddenly in his arms against the nakedness of his body and said, 'You know damn well what I want.'

She did, and there wasn't a doubt of it. But as his fingers fumbled at the back of her bikini top she whispered in protest. '*Thad*—no! You can't—here!'

The hook parted, and he pulled at the string halter and said, 'I can!'

The scrap of material fell to the ground, and he pulled her down on to the grass, too, his hands starting soft, hot waves of excitement in her.

Breathlessly, she whispered, 'Your parents!'

'They won't come out here,' he said. 'Shut up.'

His lips followed where his hands had been, and she gave a long, soft shuddering sigh and gave herself up to the strange familiarity of his touch. When his fingers found the strings at her hips, she was far and away beyond any protest.

As Thad drove them back home through the melting warmth of the night, Vanessa relived those torrid moments by the pool. He had hardly been gentle, and she was aware that her body ached a little and was probably bruised. She didn't mind that—in her own way she had been just as impatient as he, just as quick to reach the ultimate moment of sensual fulfilment.

But afterwards, she would have liked to stay held in his arms a little while, coming down to earth gradually with all the mutual tenderness that they had bypassed in their passionate flaring after months of abstinence.

Instead, she had been left, almost immediately, lying alone on the grass, while Thad rose and plunged back into the pool, coming out to rub himself down quickly, and almost brusquely tell her to get dressed as he pulled on his own trousers and fastened the belt.

He seemed impatient and almost angry, and as she dressed she shivered, feeling suddenly cold in spite of the sultry night. He didn't touch her as they walked back to the house. Going up the steps to the verandah, she started and almost tripped as a big green moth flew almost into her face, illuminated in the light from the hall. Thad shot out a hand to steady her, but dropped it almost immediately when he saw she was all right. As they said goodbye to his parents who were watching TV in the lounge, he seemed to be avoiding her eyes.

When they got home Vanessa had a shower and got ready for bed. She found Thad already in bed when she came into the bedroom. The light on his side of the bed was out, and he was lying with his eyes closed. She didn't think he was asleep, but when she lay beside him, watching his face, he didn't stir, and after a few minutes she switched off her own light and settled back, sighing, into the pillow.

She must have dropped off into sleep quite quickly. The next thing she was conscious of was waking with a faint streak of dawn lightening the drapes across the window. She didn't know why she had wakened so early, but a quick glance at Thad showed her in the dim light that his eyes were open. He was lying back with his head pillowed on his hands, staring into space, and there was a faint frown between his dark brows. His arms were bare, without a pyjama jacket.

She lay looking at him, realising that he didn't know she was awake, too. He looked as though he might have been lying there like that a long time. She wondered what he was thinking about. He didn't look happy. Memory stirred, and she felt a faint, desolate aching in her throat. Last night should have made everything all right. But still she knew something was missing, some vital factor had been lost from their marriage during Thad's time in the hospital. The encounter by the pool should have helped to heal the wounds, but even then there had been some basic ingredient left out. It had, in the end, been something less than love.

She moved softly and felt a place on her arm that throbbed faintly, and her fingers touched a slight, swelling hardness that she knew was a bruise, because Thad had not really cared much, last night, if he hurt her. He hadn't, she knew, cared about anything very much except his own satisfaction, and he had pursued that with a ruthlessness that she had never experienced before in him. That he had brought her pleasure too had been almost accidental, a product of her own love and longing for him, that had been stored up and waiting for him to release it.

Disturbed by her movement, he turned his head. Sudden longing leaped along her nerves, and she smiled and said, 'You bruised me last night.' She pulled down the sheet and touched the spot again. 'See?'

In the darkness he couldn't have seen much, perhaps a faintly darker shadow on her skin, but he looked down rather broodingly and said, 'I'm sorry.' His voice sounded curt and not at all remorseful.

Vanessa moved the tiniest bit closer to him, the smile still on her lips, and said, 'Are you really?' Her hand didn't have far to go to his bare chest, under the blankets, and she spread her fingers on his warm skin and began moving them over it, down to the waistband of pyjamas.

This time, the first fierceness of that long separation would be over. This time, she prayed, let there be tenderness.

Thad's eyes were dark and unfathomable, and he took her wandering hand in his and moved and turned until he was poised over her.

'Sorry isn't enough,' she told him, softly teasing.

His voice was deep and husky. 'What do you want me to do about it?' he asked with a slightly mocking note.

Softly she suggested, 'You could kiss it better?'

'You're asking for it, aren't you?' he said, equally softly. Had she imagined the slightly jeering note in his voice? Anxiously she stared up at his face, but the shadows were too deep for her to see it properly.

'Asking for what?' she whispered, half in fear.

He stayed looking down at her a moment longer, and a faint shiver ran through her as she realised how helpless she was if he chose to exert his strength ...

Her tiny, panicky movement of withdrawal was far too late. Thad's mouth was suddenly plundering hers with a possessive force that gave her no place to escape to, no way to hide her instinctive response to him. His hard body imprisoned her and his hands played havoc with her senses, impatient with the flimsy garment that was really no barrier anyway. A small regret for the tenderness he seemed no longer capable of giving her flickered and died in a wave of pure, primitive passion as his hands and his mouth explored her with a sureness and skill that told her he knew exactly what she really wanted ...

But when the passion had spent itself and Thad again abruptly left her without a word, she lay alone with her regret, the ache becoming stronger until it was almost a palpable grief, and the tears burned her cheeks and fell softly on to her pillow. She wondered if there would ever be tenderness again ...

She got up before her alarm went off, because she was awake, anyway, and there was no pleasure in lying in bed wondering what Thad was doing. When she had dressed she made the bed and then went out to the kitchen.

Thad had obviously made himself some toast and had finished eating. He sat at the table with the morning paper spread out in front of him, a crumb-spattered plate and an emptied teacup pushed to one side.

'You were up early,' she commented evenly, determined not to make it sound accusing or petulant.

'I got used to being woken early in the hospital,' he answered.

'Would you like a proper breakfast?'

'If I wanted it, I would have cooked it.'

She turned away and took a cup from the cupboard, depositing it on the bench with a little thud.

Thad said, 'As you're the breadwinner at the moment, do *you* want a cooked breakfast?'

'Are you offering to make it for me?' Vanessa spooned instant coffee into her cup.

'If you like.'

She turned to see how serious he was. He looked as though he meant it, all right. She said, 'I'll just have toast, thanks.'

He got up and started to make it for her, and she put some sugar in her cup and sat down, watching.

Thad pushed down the lever on the toaster and looked up, catching her eye. 'Fair division of labour,' he said gently. 'I'm told I can't work yet, so until I can get another job, the housework is my responsibility—okay?'

'Okay,' she said weakly.

She saw that the page of the paper he had been perusing was the Help Wanted column.

'Thad, wouldn't they take you back in the Department?' she asked hesitantly.

'Not as a surveyor,' he said. 'My eyesight isn't good enough for the job, now. And I'm told that climbing and walking a lot are taboo for a good long while. All the rugged work was what I liked most. I don't fancy sitting at a desk juggling figures and drawing plans all day.'

'I see. There aren't many jobs in this area, Thad.'

'No. We may have to move.' She looked up quickly, and he said almost roughly, 'Will you mind so much?'

'I—I don't know,' she said. 'I'd got used to the idea of staying here, I suppose. Anyway, we don't have to think about it until—until something comes up, do we?'

'That's right. You can bury your head a bit longer, little ostrich.'

His smile was slightly unkind, and she looked away. She heard the click of the toaster, and a few moments later he had put a plate in front of her holding two slices, thickly buttered as she liked them.

'What will you do today?' she asked.

He was leaning against the bench, arms folded. 'I have certain—plans,' he said cryptically. 'I may do some shopping, later. Do you want anything?'

'I don't think so. I stocked up last week, when I knew you were coming home.

'Very provident of you. What do we eat tonight?'

'Are you cooking?'

'I can, you know.'

'I know you can. There's steak, chops, and sausages in the freezer. Please yourself.' She wanted to ask what he was going shopping for, but perhaps it was connected with his mysterious 'plans'. Or perhaps he really had no plans, and was trying to assure her that he would be occupied.

When she was ready to go to work, Thad was just drying the breakfast dishes, and she hovered in the kitchen doorway for a few minutes until he looked up, holding a tea-towel in one hand and a cup in the other.

'I'm just off to work,' she said. 'This is a reversal of the usual scene, isn't it?' she smiled.

He put down the cup and the tea-towel and went towards her. 'We haven't had time to establish any *usual* scenes,' he said.

'I meant the stock domestic scene,' she explained.

'I see.' He was standing close to her, his arm resting on the door frame. 'Well, they tell me the roles of the sexes are rapidly reversing—or merging, anyway. All the same, I don't intend this to be a permanent arrangement, so make the most of it while it lasts.' He paused. 'Are you going to kiss me goodbye?'

She grazed his chin briefly with her lips, and he put up a hand quickly and caught at her chin. She thought he was going to kiss her properly, but he examined her face as though looking for flaws, and then said, 'I suppose I'd better respect your make-up,' and let her go.

Out on the street, she walked briskly, conscious of feeling happier than she had since Thad had come home. This morning he had been much more like the man she had married, although she still sensed a quality of reserve in him, as though a part of him had been deliberately closed off from her. But one barrier, at least, had been overcome this weekend. In time she would breach the others, too.

She turned the corner on to the main road, and a sleek mustard yellow car drew up beside her, interrupting the train of her thoughts.

The passenger door opened and Ross Bray called, 'Going my way, Vanessa?'

Vanessa slid in beside him and closed the door. 'You'd want to know why, if I wasn't, wouldn't you?' she smiled. 'It was kind of you to let me have the day off on Friday, Ross. Thank you.'

'How is your husband?'

'Quite well. He won't be working yet, until the doctor has cleared him completely, in about two weeks' time, if all goes well. But he certainly seems to have recovered.'

'Good.' She thought the glance he passed over her was unusually keen. 'Let's hope things continue to progress satisfactorily.'

He was smiling a little, and it teased a long-buried memory somewhere in her brain ...

Impatiently, she turned her head to look out at the street, the old wooden shops with their verandahs shading the pavement interspersed with newer buildings of concrete and glass. The children were on their way to school, many of them barefoot in the summer, both Maori and Pakeha. They passed the school itself, where Vanessa had spent her own primary school days, the three-roomed building now augmented by a new wing of three more.

She quite liked the little country town—the whole district, in fact. Her two years in Australia and a brief period living in Auckland had not diminished her love for her home. But if Thad wanted to move ...

She would regret leaving the little house so soon, though. They had put a lot of time into getting it just right before the wedding, a lot of their hopes and dreams had gone into that house. Everything had been going so well ... When she and Thad had become engaged, there were problems, because Vanessa had come home from Australia only that year to help nurse her father, who was very ill. She had told Thad they might have to wait, since she wouldn't let her mother down, but when he obtained a transfer from Auckland to this district it seemed that she could still spend most of the days with her parents even after her marriage. Then they had found the house, and there seemed no reason to wait too long for their marriage.

'Here we are.' Ross drew up the car in his labelled parking space beside the bank, and she thanked him for the ride and opened the door. There was really no need for him to pick her up, and sometimes she wished he wouldn't. In fact, she left the house deliberately at irregular times, sometimes early, sometimes giving herself barely sufficient time to walk the distance, when she was staying at the house, and had been glad to have the excuse that she was often living at her mother's, when Ross suggested picking her up regularly, as he was passing.

For one thing, the gossip in a small town could be wildly wrong, but it usually had some basis in one or two solid facts, however innocent. Vanessa had been the victim of gossip once before, and she knew how hurt her parents had been by it. She was well aware that her devotion to her father had redeemed her in the district's eyes, and although she didn't particularly care what people said about her, and in her younger days had virtually thumbed her nose at rumour and speculation, for her family's sake and for Thad's family, too, she preferred not to fuel any now.

Another reason was the one small fact that had lain at the heart of the stories six years ago. She had been, once, head over heels in love with Ross Bray, when she was an eighteen-year-old innocent, pretty and popular and sure of herself in her own limited little country world, but quite out of her depth with a handsome, self-assured and terribly attractive, sophisticated young man from the city.

Ross Bray had once broken her heart, and it had taken

a long time for her to pick up the pieces again. She had no fear of her heart being endangered again, since she had firmly given it into Thad's keeping, but she also wanted to be quite sure that Ross didn't have the idea he might be able to affect her the way he once had. What she had told Bret was true—she believed that Ross had changed and was really trying to help her and make up for some of the misery he had caused her. But she was also aware that he still found her very attractive, and the slightest sign of encouragement would be disastrous.

She knew she was walking a tightrope. She wanted the job at the bank, so she needed to be pleasant and friendly to Ross. She didn't want him getting the wrong idea, so she had to be slightly distant and not *too* friendly. So far, she had managed the tightrope well.

CHAPTER SIX

VANESSA put away her handbag and walked to her desk, smiling a little as she noticed the two juniors watching Ross stride into his office. They were both quite nice-looking girls, with the freshness of youth, but Ross scarcely knew their names. It didn't stop him from occasionally teasing them in a masculine way, or giving them his gorgeous smile when he noticed they were about, but that was for him an automatic reflex. He had given up collecting girls—*and you two don't know how lucky you are*! Vanessa thought wryly.

They wouldn't have stood a chance, just as she hadn't, at eighteen. How stupidly sure she had been that everything Ross said to her, every touch, every smile, was for her alone—that he had never loved another girl as he loved her. How trustingly she had let him make dizzying love to her, until she had no heart, no mind, no will of her own. Only lovely, loving dreams of their future together...

And then the blinding, sickening knowledge that it had all been lies, the day she overheard him talking to a friend—talking about her in a way that made her feel almost faint with shame. And then comparing her with other girls that he and his friend both knew—other girls just as foolish and infatuated and idiotically trusting, she supposed, as she had been.

For a time she had wanted nothing but to die, just quietly, where no one would find her. Instead she had gone back home, to her parents and a small-town job in the county council office, and just when life was nearly back to normal, and she had begun to laugh again and look back on the experience with remembered humiliation, but a certain acceptance of a lesson that was hard but valuable, Ross had been transferred by the bank to Aputa.

She had snubbed his attempts to see her again, several times, and not without a certain satisfaction. And then one night at a party he had managed to get her alone in a secluded corner of someone's garden, and at first she had been frightened, because she remembered the effect his merest touch had used to have on her, and might have again...

She threatened to scream when he took her in his arms, but he only laughed, his handsome face triumphant and confident. And it wasn't much use screaming, because it was a fairly boisterous party and there was a lot of screaming going on, anyway, apart from the blaring music from amplified recordings.

Vanessa tried to fight him off, until he hurt her, and then she tried instead to be passive and unresponsive as he kissed her in the old way...

And to her own surprise she found that it was easy—in her mind she played back, like a recording, all that he had said about her to his friend, and her body stayed cold and unrelenting, while his kisses grew more passionate and his breath quickened, and she knew with an incredulous mixture of cold triumph and overwhelming relief that he wanted her, but she definitely didn't want him. Not in any way.

And when she told him, coldly and finally and with a steady voice and perfect control of her breath and her emotions, that he no longer had any power to move her, he looked so stunned that it was funny, and she laughed.

That was a mistake. Not many girls had resisted Ross. And none of them had laughed when they did it. She had thought for a moment that he would hit her, and wondered afterwards if he would have, if another couple had not at that moment wandered their way.

Instead he had brushed past her on his way back to the party, and she had heard him mutter savagely, '*You'll be sorry, Vanessa!*'

At the time she had thought it just an empty threat, because he had been thoroughly worsted and was determined to have the last word. But it had been more than that, she thought with dismay when she finally heard the rumours. He had really meant it...

'No, I didn't mean it!' he had said six years later, when he came and offered her the job at the bank. 'I know that—afterwards—you must have thought I'd—well, spread stories about you on purpose. But it wasn't like that, believe me.'

'It was coincidence, then?' she asked with faint sarcasm.

'No. I can't pretend it wasn't my fault, and I'm deeply sorry—even ashamed.'

'Isn't this apology—if that's what it is—a little late, Ross?'

'Yes. But I don't think you would have listened to me before—as I hope you're going to listen to me now.'

Vanessa took a deep breath. 'All right.'

'I was furious when I left you at the party—you know that. I know what you thought of me in those days, and I daresay I deserved it. But believe me, you were never just another girl to me, Vanessa. You were special.'

'After I walked out on you—yes. I must have been different.'

'Please don't! You were always different.'

'That wasn't the impression that I got when I heard you telling Bob about—us.'

'Oh, Vanessa! It was man talk. It didn't mean anything! All men talk when they're together——'

'*Some* men might.'

'My God! You're almost as innocent now as you were then, aren't you?'

'I wasn't so innocent by the time you—*Oh*! This is getting us nowhere——'

'No, it isn't. Just listen for a minute, will you—please, Vanessa?'

Vanessa closed her lips and nodded.

'I know you don't believe me, but I was in love with you. When I was transferred here, and saw you again, it seemed fate was presenting me with a second chance—a chance I didn't deserve, but nevertheless I was determined to take it. I didn't blame you for being a bit cold—knowing you felt I'd treated you badly. When I kissed you at that party and found you really meant it when you said it was all over, I was—pretty upset.'

'You mean, when I laughed at you, you were pretty mad.'

'Well—that too.' He laughed himself, ruefully. 'At that time, I'll admit, I was a fairly shallow character. I guess my parents spoiled me as a kid. I was the only child, and not only that, but the only boy in my generation of the family. My grandfather saw me as the golden hope of the family. Anything my parents couldn't afford, he bought for me. And when I got interested in girls—well, it may sound vain, but I've never had to do much chasing.'

Vanessa believed that. Ross had not only looks but charm and wit as well. 'Are you saying you're different now?' she asked.

'I'm saying everyone has to grow up some time. I was still rather juvenile, I'm afraid, even at twenty-three. That night I drowned my sorrow in too much drink—and not alone. I'm afraid that a new acquaintance begins to look like a bosom pal in certain circumstances.'

'So you indulged in some more "man talk"?'

Ross nearly winced. 'Look, it wasn't like that other time, believe me. I was genuinely upset. I admit I said some bitter things about you. I had hoped that now I'd found you again, maybe we could get together again. Because I *loved* you, and this time I wanted things to be better. But you'd turned me down, and I was miserable. Honestly, Vanessa, I swore the man to secrecy. I was new to the district, remember—how was I to know he was the boy most likely to tell the world?'

'It didn't take long to get around,' she said bitterly. 'Of course, it was quite some time before *I* got to hear the stories that were circulating about me. I suppose I was the last to know. Oh, I'd got the message, all right, about the sort of girl I was supposed to be—from every man who took me out. But I didn't recognise the signals. I thought I was finding out what men were really like. It was very disillusioning. I didn't realise, you see, that the decent men were avoiding me.'

'Vanessa!' His voice was low. 'I don't have any right to ask, but can you ever forgive me?'

'I don't know,' she said. 'You know, from what I *did* finally manage to find out—about what was being said—some of the—the details were fairly imaginative.'

Ross passed his hand over his eyes. 'Oh, my dear! I swear to you I had no idea—you know how gossip grows and gets embellished as it travels.'

'Yes.' She did know, and she knew it was impossible now to ever be sure just what had happened six years ago, how much had been due to malice or to thoughtlessness, and which details had originated with Ross.

Certainly Ross seemed genuinely remorseful now, and anxious to make amends. And she did need a way of making money, while Thad remained in hospital. Eventually there would be a payment from the Accident Compensation Fund, she supposed, but red tape seemed to take forever to get unravelled.

'If—I take the job,' she said carefully, 'do you—personally—expect anything in return?'

She watched his face, and his eyes were quite steady on hers as he promised, 'No strings, Vanessa. You don't have to do a thing except your job.'

And it had worked out. She couldn't help but be aware that Ross sometimes looked at her in a way that made it plain he still found her very attractive. He might have grown up, but she didn't think he would ever grow out of that particular way of looking at women—he had a practised eye. But only once had he followed it up, and although the incident had not been quite as easily dealt with as she had led Bret to believe, she had coped. And she still had her job.

Ross drove her home after work. He had often offered, but usually she made some excuse—she had shopping to do or was going to visit her sister. Or sometimes she brought her own car if she had been running late in the morning, or had a lot of shopping to do. Sometimes she shopped for her mother, and of course at least half the time she had actually been living at the farm rather than her own and Thad's home.

She accepted Ross's offer of a lift because she was eager to get home as soon as she could, now that Thad was there.

Once she had felt like that about the man sitting beside her now, she recalled with something like surprise. Now there was—nothing. As he swung the car around the corner, she looked at his handsome profile. He hadn't changed very much, really, to look at. His hair was still dark brown and crisply curly, his eyes blue with long dark lashes, his nose classically straight. She supposed, to a stranger, he would be just as good-looking as Thad. Certainly he had bowled her over when she had first seen him. For a while she had been a fervent believer in love at first sight. But it was a shortlived love that died with disillusion, when she had woken up finally to the fact that the man she had thought endowed with every virtue—or every one that counted, anyway—was a fake.

It had made her very wary when Thad began to show an interest in her. Because Thad too had a decided air of rather overwhelming masculine attraction, a way of looking at a woman that made her realise very consciously that she *was* a woman, and a certain expertise that she well knew was acquired by the practice he had had with a number of the prettiest girls in the district and farther afield. Thad, too, had found no necessity to do much chasing where girls were concerned. When he first began to show an interest in Vanessa Morris, her sole desire, after her first instinct to succumb to his charm, his looks, his undoubted sex-appeal, had been to run—as far and as fast as she could.

But this time Thad had done some running, and in the end he convinced her he was serious, and she realised that in spite of his outward similarity to Ross Bray, the man beneath the charm and the surface good looks was a real man, and could give her far more than Ross had ever been able to—or ever wanted to.

Ross drew up outside the house and interrupted her reverie. 'Why the intense stare?' he asked, and she realised she had been caught out, still looking at him.

'Oh, sorry,' she smiled placatingly. 'I was just thinking you haven't changed much since I first knew you.'

'I have, you know,' he said softly. 'I thought I'd convinced you of that.'

'I meant in looks,' she said.

'Neither have you—except to grow more beautiful,' he said.

'Thank you.' Vanessa acknowledged the compliment coolly and turned to open the door.

'They tell me Thad is scarred,' said Ross, making her look back at him. 'Is it bad?'

'No, it isn't bad. I expect rumour exaggerates as usual.'

'Probably. You'll be living here permanently now, I take it. No more skating off to your mother's every other week?'

'That's right. I have a husband here, now.'

'Would your husband mind, then, if I picked you up and took you to work in the mornings?'

'Thad isn't jealous,' she said carefully. 'He has no reason to be.'

'Then——?'

'I don't think so, thank you, Ross. It isn't far to walk, and I quite enjoy the exercise.'

'And rumour exaggerates, is that it?'

'Well, that too, perhaps. I do have reason to be wary of rumour.'

'That was below the belt, Vanessa.'

'I'm sorry, I didn't mean to bring up old grievances.'

'I forgive you. I don't see what even the most inveterate gossip could make of a ride in a car for five minutes down the main street of the town, though. Do you?'

'No, you're probably right. But I'd still rather not.'

For a moment she thought a flicker of annoyance showed in his blue eyes. Then he shrugged and smiled at her with all his considerable charm and said, 'Okay. It's your choice. If that's the way you want it . . .'

'Thank you for understanding, Ross. Goodnight.'

'Goodnight.'

When she went in, she felt a stab of pleasure that she could go around to the back door and find it unlocked and walk in to see Thad there, instead of using her key and going in the front way. It made it so much more normal—more like really coming home, rather than just to a house.

The kitchen was empty except for a pot of potatoes gently steaming on the stove, and the bench littered with preparations.

She went into the hall and called, 'Thad! Are you home?'

He called from the lounge, and she went in, vaguely disappointed that he had not come out to greet her. He was standing in front of the window that looked out on the road, with his back to it, hands in pockets. His face was hard to see against the late afternoon light, but there was a kind of tenseness about his stance, so that her first impulse to go to him and put her arms about him faltered, and she stood uncertainly in the doorway instead.

'You're early,' he commented.

'Only a little. I got a lift home.'

'With the boss, no less. I saw you from the window.'

Vanessa walked into the room, swinging down her bag from her shoulder, holding the strap bunched in her hand. Lightly she enquired, 'Were you watching for me?'

'I heard the car.'

'I see.' She didn't, quite.

'You were a long time coming in.'

'Not very long, surely. Five minutes?' she guessed. 'We were talking.'

'So I gathered. Don't you get enough time to talk at work? Or was this a private conversation?'

'Not particularly,' she answered, but without particular confidence. She was vaguely surprised and uneasy. 'Thad, you're not *jealous*, are you?' she asked. Almost to herself, she added, 'I told him you're not jealous.'

There was a heartbeat's silence, just time enough for her to wonder why on earth she had said that, to realise what a number of misconstructions were possible on a remark like that. Then Thad's voice came flatly: 'Did you indeed? I wonder why.'

But he didn't stay to find out, just walked past her without another word. And when she said, 'Thad——' and made to stop him he kept walking so that her hand grazed off his sleeve and fell to her side.

Slowly Vanessa went to the bedroom and put away her bag. She pulled the pins out of her hair and brushed it out and then combed it back behind her ears. Then she went into the kitchen where Thad was busy turning a couple of steaks in a marinade, and said, 'Shall I set the table?'

'If you like.' He looked up indifferently.

Taking the knives and forks from their drawer, she said, 'Ross offered to pick me up for work every morning. I said no.'

He looked up briefly and said with soft sarcasm, 'Well, good for you!'

Still holding the cutlery in her hand, she faced him challengingly. 'What's that supposed to mean?'

'It means I'm not as stupid as you seem to think,' he said.

Her eyes widened. 'You *are* jealous!'

'Is that what you want?'

'No!' She didn't understand him. 'What do you mean?'

'Yesterday a tête-à-tête with Bret. Now a cosy little chat in Ross Bray's car. And aren't you deliberately tantalising me with these fascinating snippets from that conversation? 'He offered to pick me up every morning' and 'I told him you're not jealous'—what are you trying to prove? That other men find you attractive? Or are you attempting to titillate my interest? There's no need, you know. I find you bloody nearly irresistible myself.'

Bewildered by his attack, groping for some weapon to defend herself, she said, 'You told me the other day you didn't—find me attractive any more.'

'Unfortunately,' he shrugged, 'it didn't last. Is that why you're playing games, Vanessa? To pay me out for what I said? If that's it, I warn you—call it quits now. Because I play rough.'

She looked with shock into his dark face and saw that he meant it.

'But you're wrong!' she protested. 'You have everything twisted, Thad.'

Impatiently he turned away and began putting the steak on a grill rack.

'Oh, what's the use!' Vanessa snapped angrily, and throwing down the things she was holding, so that they clattered on to the bench, she hurried down the hallway to the bedroom and slammed the door.

And that was stupid! she told herself a few minutes later when she was slightly calmer. Throwing tantrums never helped anybody. She should have stayed calm and reasoned with him.

Not that he was acting very reasonably—the accident and his prolonged stay in the hospital seemed to have upset his equilibrium.

She sat on the bed, trying to think calmly and sensibly, a long time. Hearing Thad's footsteps coming down the hallway, she tensed. The door opened, and he stood leaning against the framework.

'Are you coming to eat?' he asked calmly.

It would be childish not to. She rose and walked to the door, hesitating briefly as she reached him, trying to read his face, but it was shuttered against her. She wanted to touch him, but didn't know how he would react.

Then he moved back into the hall, and the moment was gone. She followed him to the kitchen.

The steak was delicious, and to her faint surprise, Vanessa found that she was hungry.

'That was lovely,' she said, pushing away her plate and breaking the strained silence.

'Thanks.' Thad inclined his head in acknowledgement.

'Like some peaches and ice cream?'

'Yes, please, just a little.' She sounded incredibly polite.

Hospital hadn't impaired his appetite, she noticed, watching him heap his own plate after serving her.

'What did you do today?' she asked, slicing one of her peaches with her spoon.

'I went looking for a potter,' he said.

Puzzled, she looked up at him. 'A potter? You wanted to buy some pottery?'

'No. I wanted to talk to a potter.'

'The butcher or the baker wouldn't do?' she asked, glad to see a glimmer of a smile fleetingly touch his mouth at that.

'The baker might have done at a pinch,' he said with faint amusement. 'But I prefer a genuine potter.'

'I didn't know you were interested in the craft,' she said, more than slightly at sea.

'I did learn something about it, years ago at school,' he told her. 'We had an art teacher who was keen on potting and clay sculpture. My mother has a couple of my efforts lying around the house somewhere to this day.'

'She told me you were good at art, I remember. She said once you'd wanted to be an artist.'

'Boyhood ambitions are apt to be glamorous and short-lived.'

'Well, did you find your potter?'

'I did. I got a lot of useful information, some clay, and, most important, permission to rent the use of a kiln—to fire my pottery.'

'Yours?' Bereft of any more speech, Vanessa stared at him.

Abruptly Thad stood up. 'Wait—I'll show you something.'

She heard him go into their bedroom, and a few minutes later he came out with a shoebox in his hands. He put it down on the table and removed the lid, taking out two smallish objects wrapped in tissue. He removed the wrappings from them and stood the two clay figures on the table.

One was, she thought at first, a bird, with hunched wings and a predatory look. Then, as she picked it up, she saw that it was a human figure, but with sharp, hunched shoulders and a beaky nose—it was clever, and a little sinister.

She looked at Thad enquiringly and picked up the other figure. This one was short and round, wearing something vaguely resembling a coat, with a head that was round and unmistakably porcine.

'Oh, Thad!' she said, half laughing, half in protest. 'Poor Doctor Price!'

'You do recognise him, then?'

'Of course. Who is the other one?'

'The vulture? Miss Henshaw, in charge of occupational therapy at the hospital.'

'That's where you did these?'

'Of course.'

'I thought you despised occupational therapy.'

'I did. But Miss Henshaw is a tough old bird, and determined as well. When I told her in no uncertain terms what she could do with her basketry and weaving, she ripped back at me with a few choice words of her own, threw a chunk of clay at me, and told me that she personally didn't give a hoot in hell if I never regained the full use of my hand, and invited me to see if I could push the clay about, because she wasn't going to let me do it to her. I made that thing as a sort of revenge and left it on the bench for her to find, hoping it would annoy her.'

'And did it?'

'Apparently not. It was gone the next day, and nothing was said. She gave me some more clay to play with without a word, and I thought she'd thrown it out and decided to ignore the whole thing. I fooled about a bit, then I began to get the feel of the clay, and got interested in seeing what I could do with it. Not pots—I'm not interested in that part of it—at least, not just now. But this kind of thing, and some straight animal figures. Then one day she brought in someone else—a friend of hers who runs a handcraft shop in Auckland. She'd got him to look at the one I did of her, and a couple of others she snaffled when I wasn't looking—things were always disappearing in the therapy room, I hadn't thought anything of it. They'd got them fired for me. And he wanted to know if I was interested in selling him some.'

'You never told me any of this!'

Suddenly his face assumed the shuttered look again. 'I'm telling you now,' he said. Then, relenting slightly, he added, 'It could have been a fluke—a flash in the pan. But apparently Rogers—the shop owner—doesn't think so. He sold all that I made before. Now he wants more.'

'Oh, Thad——' Vanessa picked up the little vulture-figure of Miss Henshaw and ran her fingers over its contours. 'It could be a whole new career for you.'

'Don't build your dreams too high,' Thad warned. 'That's why I didn't tell you before. A few sales don't make a fortune. And I still have a lot to learn—particularly about the technical side. I went to the library today, too. I don't even know how to work a kiln.'

'It's lucky you found one, isn't it?' she said eagerly. 'It's almost a stroke of fate.'

'The accident was a stroke of fate, too,' he reminded her grimly. 'One that I could have done without.'

'Where will you work?' Vanessa asked.

'The spare bedroom will do. We haven't much furniture in there, anyway. I'll need a second-hand table, and a good supply of clay. I found today there are several potters in the area, and I got some good advice on sources of supply.'

'You may not need to look for another job, after all. Then we could stay here, couldn't we?'

Thad had been fingering the pig-like effigy of Dr Price, but now he looked up sharply, and then said in an oddly expressionless voice, 'Is that what you want? To stay here?'

'Don't you?'

He put down the clay figure and said, 'I don't really care, one way or the other.'

He picked up the plates and began stacking them.

He made love to her that night with the same merciless passion as before, but this time he stayed lying in the bed beside her afterwards, not touching her, but lying staring at the ceiling. When she put out tentative fingers and touched the scar on his cheek, he pushed her hand roughly away. That night the raw ache in her heart began to harden into bitterness.

Thad bought supplies, and had the spare room fixed up with a big old pine table that had once graced a farm kitchen and had then been relegated to the corner of a garage. It wasn't beautiful, but it was ideal for Thad's purpose. He put up some shelves and they began to fill with a respectable collection of his 'clay cartoons' as he called them. Some of them were of political figures and well-known personalities, and to Vanessa's inexpert eye they looked very good.

One night when she arrived home from work she heard voices from his workroom, and, curious, pushed wide the nearly closed door. Thad was sitting at his work table, and leaning across him, her hand on his shoulder, and her other hand guiding his as it slid carefully across a hunk of clay with some sort of wire tool, was a girl.

She had long red hair that was brushing against Thad's neck, and faintly freckled golden skin. She was wearing a long muslin dress that was pulled in under full, voluptuous breasts with a coloured ribbon.

'There!' she said, as a curl of clay fell to the table in the wake of the wire tool. 'Now do you see?'

'I do, thanks.'

The girl straightened and saw Vanessa standing in the doorway. Unselfconsciously, she smiled and said, 'Hallo. I didn't hear you come in.'

Thad turned and stood up. 'This is Vanessa, Celine. Celine Hudson, Vanessa, who owns the kiln that I've been using. She's been kind enough to give me a few hints.'

The two girls shook hands, and Vanessa couldn't help answering the wide, friendly smile that was directed at her.

'Your husband has talent,' Celine said.

'I expect you have too,' Vanessa answered politely.

'Not for his sort of thing. That's something unique. I do pots, mostly.'

'I see. You won't be in competition, then. Well, if you two are working, I don't want to disturb you——'

Thad had been standing silently by, watching them both, and feeling her presence was not really wanted, Vanessa made to withdraw, but Celine stopped her. 'Oh, no, don't let me drive you away. What's the time? I must have been here *hours*!' She turned and caught Thad's wrist to look at his watch. 'Heavens! I had no idea——'

'Stay and eat with us,' invited Thad. 'You don't have to go home, do you?'

'Well, I don't have a man to cook for at the moment,'

Celine admitted. 'But—Vanessa——'

'I'm chief cook at the moment,' Thad told her firmly. 'Come and help me make a meal.'

They went towards the kitchen, Thad's hand on Celine's shoulder. Vanessa went slowly into the bedroom to put away her bag and change her shoes. She felt tired and a trifle sticky. It had been a busy day at work, and her feet ached. There was another ache somewhere, too, that had started when she saw how casually Thad had put his arm about Celine. It was a long time since he had done that with *her*.

On impulse, she decided to have a shower and change her clothes completely. The water refreshed her, and she made up her face carefully again and put on a cool flounced skirt and peasant-style blouse, so that she looked casual and fresh.

Celine was good company, vivacious and natural. Vanessa remembered seeing her about in Aputa a few times, but had never spoken to her. Now she learned that the girl lived in a cottage on one of the farms nearby. 'It belongs to a cousin, and the rent is cheap. Ritchie fixed me up a small kiln, and I'm happy with my potting until he comes home. Ritchie's a merchant sailor,' she explained. 'He's away about six months of the year.' She smiled. 'Oh, when he comes home, I'm such a dutiful little wife—you wouldn't believe——!' She gestured with her hands and laughed. 'I cook meals and serve them on time, wash his shirts—all the slippers and pipe bit. And then, just as it's about to drive me mad, he's off to sea again, and I'm as free as a bird—and hating it, would you believe. Moping around because Ritchie's gone. Oh, it's a great old life, I can tell you.'

Vanessa laughed, too. 'You must be the ideal sailor's wife,

glad to see him leave and glad to see him come home.'

'We muddle along. The thing is, neither of us was really ready to settle down when we married. Only we couldn't bear to let each other go, either. It's worked out well.'

When Celine had gone, driving off in a battered VW of uncertain vintage, Vanessa commented, as Thad closed the door, 'What a nice person she is.'

'Yes. That's what I thought when I met her. She seems so—honest.'

That night was the first in a long time that he did not make love to her. Vanessa felt guilty to realise she was relieved.

The doctors had cleared Thad for work, with certain warnings about heavy physical activity and doing too much, but already he had made some modest profit from his clay figures, and it seemed possible he could make a living from it before too long. He spent long hours turning out more work, and Vanessa was taking a share in the housework again, now. They were both working and busy, and on the surface their life was relatively tranquil. Thad was still inclined to be irritable at times, but most of the time he was simply—aloof.

It hurt that the closeness they had once shared seemed to have evaporated. Even when Thad made love to her, it was done silently and almost reluctantly, as though he drew her to him and held her in his arms because he couldn't help himself, as though he hated himself—and her—even while he parted her lips with his deep, seeking kisses, and his fingers traced the secret places that brought her shuddering to passionate life beneath his hands, making her abandon herself to whatever he wanted of her.

And there was never any sweetness in the aftermath,

only the bitter knowledge that her love held her prisoner, making her a slave to his unloving passion.

Bret and Clementina came to see them one Sunday afternoon when they were staying with Thad's parents.

'Is this one of yours?' Clem asked, as she picked up a chunky ceramic cat that sat on the top of the stereogram in the lounge. 'I hear you're doing very well.'

'Not bad,' Thad answered. 'That's one of my early ones.'

'Where do you keep the rest? Or do you sell them as quickly as they're made?'

'I have a respectable stock in the spare room just now,' said Thad. 'I'm looking for new outlets now, actually. My first contact, George Rogers, is slightly over-stocked, and there's only one small local shop here, that's taken some on a commission basis.'

'May I see what you have?' asked Clem. 'I might be interested.'

'For your boutique?' Thad raised his brows. 'I thought you only sold clothes.'

'And some accessories. I have the type of clientele who just might be interested in some unusual pottery—I might start a small corner for it. Have you thought of bracelets, necklaces, pendants—even belts, of pottery ware? We're getting some very interesting stuff—most of it imported. It's popular.'

Thad stood up and waved her ahead of him. 'My lovely Clem, you inspire me. Come into my parlour and I'll show you your heart's desire.'

Clem gave him one of her typical, mocking smiles. 'All I want to see is your pottery, Thad.'

When they had gone Bret got up to pour himself another drink, after asking for Vanessa's permission. 'Can I get something for you?' he asked.

'No, thanks. One is enough for me.'

He came and sat beside her on the sofa, inspecting her face quizzically.

'You look tired,' he said. 'What have you been doing lately?'

'Nothing,' she shrugged. 'Going to work, coming home, eating, sleeping. Like most people.' She gave a weary little smile.

'You sound as though you're in a rut,' he said.

'Again—like most people,' she shrugged.

'Not you and Thad,' Bret said with a hint of sharpness. 'You're two of the most alive people I know—normally. What's the matter with you?'

Vanessa sighed. 'I wish I knew, Bret. Thad just seems so —so distant from me.'

'I hoped it would have come right by now,' said Bret, frowning. 'Shall I talk to him?'

'Oh, no! He'd hate it if he thought I'd confided in you —and I shouldn't have. It's a habit with me.'

'I don't mind.'

'Thad does. I don't think he's ever been convinced that you and I simply had a platonic relationship.'

'Then he's a fool!'

A little startled at his vehemence, she looked up, and he smiled ruefully. 'Sorry, Vanessa, I suppose that doesn't sound very flattering for you. I mean, I'd always regarded you as one of the neighbourhood youngsters, and I thought Thad would realise that. Also that he would take your word in any case.'

'You were very good to one of the neighbourhood youngsters, Bret. When you took me under your wing, I was really grateful. I never thought at the time—but did any of the gossip about me rebound on you?'

'Not to my knowledge. And I can cope with gossip. The trick is to ignore it.'

'You were good at that, weren't you? Going around with you as my exclusive escort for a year certainly killed my reputation as the wild girl of the district.'

'I think your own behaviour did that.'

'I could never have done it without your help, Bret. That last awful thing—the drunken driving charge——'

'It wasn't you who was the accused, you know.'

'I know. But we all felt guilty. All of us had been drinking, and it was horrible being brought into court as a witness, and having to admit that we'd drunk enough to be silly.'

'*You* weren't drunk.'

'No, but we were all in it together, Bret. I've always felt the rest of us were just as much to blame as poor Billy. The magistrate was right to tick us off for irresponsibility. Thank God no one was seriously hurt in the accident. But my poor parents, seeing the magistrate's remarks in the paper, and my name ...'

'You made it up to them, Vanessa,' he said gently. 'They couldn't have wished for a better daughter these last two years. Your father died a happy man.'

'Thank you, Bret. But I wish I'd never got mixed up with that crowd. Not because they were bad, they were really harmless, although the fun got a bit silly at times. But my parents were worried for me, and hurt.'

'Well, it was understandable at the time. *You* had been hurt badly in your first love affair—a gay, happy-go-lucky crowd must have seemed just the antidote you needed. *And* I suspect that you were thumbing your nose at the gossip that had spread about you. There was an element of "give a dog a bad name" too, wasn't there?'

'There was,' she agreed ruefully. 'You've always been very understanding, Bret.'

'Well, a lot of water has flowed since then.' He leaned closer and took her hand in his. 'I still want you to be happy, Vanessa. If there's anything I can do——'

She looked at him in gratitude, and then the door opened and he dropped her hand and sat back as Thad and Clementina returned.

Vanessa thought Thad looked at them sharply, and wished that Bret had not been holding her hand just at that moment. It had meant nothing except a gesture of genuine brotherly concern, but life with Thad had been difficult enough lately, and as she had told his brother, he had never been entirely convinced that the relationship between Vanessa and Bret had never been a romantic one.

She supposed it was not really surprising. Bret had always been a very attractive man, and he had a self-assurance born of a relaxed confidence which was in its own way as devastating as Thad's more vitally obvious masculinity. Even in the year that Vanessa had been dating no one but Bret, who had offered her his services as a refuge from hurt and despair, she had been conscious of Thad's power of attraction whenever he was about. It made her stick closely to his older brother, clinging to his protection, because she was terribly afraid of being hurt again as Ross had hurt her, afraid of giving her scarcely mended heart again to the sort of man who would break it without a second thought.

And in that year, in spite of the electric current of awareness that flowed between them, Thad had never followed it up. She had sometimes been aware of his watching her with his brother, of the wry twist of his smile as he saw her hang on Bret's arm or watched them laughing over a private joke. And she had tried to keep out of his way, because he disturbed her, and her new-found tranquillity was too precious to be disturbed.

When Bret came back from a trip to Britain with Clementina, wearing his engagement ring, at about the same time that Vanessa returned from Australia Thad had begun a pursuit of her that had alternately excited and frightened her.

They had both grown up in the district, and she knew he had taken out many girls and never been serious about any of them. Playing with fire, as she well knew, she had accepted a few of his invitations, and managed to remain outwardly cool and casual in the face of his blatantly admiring eyes and the audacious compliments he paid her, his eyes gleaming darkly under half-closed lids as he watched for her reaction.

The first time he kissed her—apart from the brief peck they had exchanged at the party her sister gave to welcome her home—had sparked off a blazing quarrel.

Knowing very well that he was not the kind of man who wanted a lengthy platonic relationship, she had deferred the moment as long as she could, unwilling to cope with the deepening of their emotions that kisses would inevitably bring, still afraid of trusting him. He had accepted her evasive tactics at first with a good grace, letting her leave him after their outings with a cool goodnight at her door, allowing his arm to slip from her shoulders when she made a movement away from his embrace. But once or twice she had caught her breath at a certain warning light in his eye, an unmistakable gleam that seemed to signal her that he would not wait for ever.

One night he took her dancing, and on the crowded floor

she had for a time relaxed her guard, allowing Thad to hold her close, his fingers lightly tracing her spine and his lips against her temple as they swayed to dreamy dance tunes. Delicious sensations invaded her body, and when the music stopped she couldn't prevent an involuntary sigh. Momentarily Thad's hold tightened, and his hand slid up her spine to her nape and lifted her face before she had time to hide what was in her eyes.

He drew a quick breath and a sudden light leaped into his dark eyes, and when he released her, instead of taking her back to their seats, he said, 'Let's go, Vanessa.'

Weakly, she obeyed his compelling hand on her waist, but the cool air outside restored a little of her common sense and control, and when Thad drew up the car under the deep shadows of some trees not far from her home, she remained sitting rigidly in her seat, staring out the windshield at the distant hills. Pale moonlight was silvering the dark, mysterious mantle of tane—the damp virgin bush covering the slopes. Thad had opened his window and the mournful low tones of a morepork owl mingled with the high shrilling of the crickets.

Thad moved his right hand from the wheel and touched her, gently turning her to face him with his strong fingers holding her face.

'Vanessa——'

His other arm came round her shoulders to draw her close, and she stiffened a little, but as his hand raised her face and her lips were found by his, she remained passive.

His mouth was cool and gentle and persuasive, and it took all her will power to resist the urge to put up her arms and bring him closer to her, to open her lips in invitation and offer him whatever kind of satisfaction it pleased him to take.

Eventually he stopped kissing her and raised his head a little to try to read her face in the darkness.

'I expected a more enthusiastic response, after that look you gave me on the dance floor,' he said quietly.

'I'm sorry—I can't oblige,' Vanessa answered, trying to sound calm and slightly chilly.

'Can't—or won't?' he asked softly, and bent his head again, touching the corners of her mouth, first one and then the other, with his lips and his tongue. It was unbearably sensual, and Vanessa jerked her head aside and pushed at him. For an instant he resisted, his arms still holding her prisoner, and then he let her go.

She moved away from him, and he said abruptly, 'Would you have pushed Bret away?'

The circumstances had never arisen with Bret, but admitting that to Thad would have made her more vulnerable to him than ever. Sharply she replied, 'That's none of your business!'

'I don't think you would have,' he stated flatly. 'For one thing, Bret isn't the type to stand for the kind of teasing you've been trying on me. He would have made you follow through.'

'Bret never *made* me do anything,' she said. His accusation of teasing was unfair enough to sting, and she added recklessly, 'Bret is too much a gentleman to force a girl into anything—and too much of a man to need to!'

'And I'm not?' Thad asked dangerously. His eyes glittered in the moonlight.

She couldn't bring herself to say no. But to say yes was dangerously close to letting him know of his power over her emotions. She contented herself with a small shrug, as though he could think what he wished.

'I'm not a gentleman,' Thad said. 'And you're no lady,

are you?' He reached across for her, and she hit out at him, her palm stinging against his cheek. He grabbed her wrists and pinned her back against the seat. 'No, you're not,' he muttered. 'You're a flesh and blood woman, Vanessa, not the lifeless statue you pretended to be when I kissed you. There's fire in your veins, not ice. I know it. And as for me being a man——' His grip on her tightened as he moved closer to her.

She tried to turn her mouth away from him, but he just laughed softly at her futile efforts as she writhed in his grasp, and then he captured it anyway. It was a darkly sensuous kiss with an edge of violence, and she suffered it in a helpless agony of wanting and hating him at the same time.

When his mouth left her lips it wandered to the warm hollow beneath her ear, nuzzling and nipping her skin, and he said, 'Kiss me back, sweet Vanessa.'

'*No!*' Restlessly, she moved her head, trying to escape him, and he released her wrists and caught her head in his hands to tilt it and ruthlessly possess her lips again. Her hands beat helplessly against his shoulders until the traitorous, mounting desire to respond to the insistence of his mouth threatened to overwhelm her. Her hands fell and tears slipped between her lids and ran from her cheeks on to his hands as he held her.

His mouth lifted from hers, and she felt his thumbs stroke the tears away. '*Don't!* he muttered. And then softly, 'I'm sorry.'

The gentleness was worse than anything, and she wrenched herself away so as not to give in to the almost irresistible impulse to lay her head down on his chest and beg him to keep on kissing her until she forgot all the good reasons why she shouldn't trust him.

She fumbled for the door handle, and he grabbed at her

wrist and said harshly, 'Don't be silly. I'm not going to rape you. I'll take you home.'

'Please!' she said.

For a moment longer his hand encircled her wrist. Then he let her go and started the car.

Afterwards Vanessa regretted that she had not told him the truth about herself and Bret then. Later, when she tried to explain, he refused to listen to her, saying it didn't matter now that they were sure of belonging to each other, and silencing her with long, pulsating kisses.

Their courtship had been stormy. She had decided after that devastating evening not to go out with Thad again, but her own heart betrayed her, and knowing she was endangering it, she couldn't help being glad when he turned up to visit her father and take her out for a drive. Although she told herself that she had no choice between his stratagems and her parents' urging to get out and have a break from nursing her father, she knew it was her own helpless attraction to him that was the deciding factor.

When he kissed her again she relaxed and responded with undisguised enjoyment. But the light of satisfaction in his eyes when he raised his head and looked down at her flushed face made her cautious again, and she said lightly, 'Is that an improvement?'

'Definitely,' he replied, veiling his eyes as his gaze lingered on her lips. 'Have you decided to trust me after all?'

Disturbed as she was by his perception, she said, deliberately obtuse, 'I never thought you would—attack me, Thad. I just objected to your taking my co-operation for granted, that's all. I've nothing against a few kisses to pass the time.'

'Is that how you think of them? Just a pleasant diversion?'

'With you—yes. We both know there's nothing serious in our relationship. We can both enjoy what it has to offer without getting too intense about it—provided you understand that I'm not—I'm not saying that I'm willing to be——'

'Available?' he supplied, somewhat drily. His face had changed subtly while she spoke, his eyes narrowing and his mouth becoming thinner, so that her airy explanation faltered into a hesitant fumbling for words at the end. Trying to recoup, she said, 'I mean that if you hope for more than kisses, you'd better look elsewhere.'

'You wouldn't—mind?' he said, with a trace of sarcasm.

Vanessa shrugged. 'It's up to you. You see, whatever you may have heard about my lurid past——'

'I'm not interested in your past!' he interrupted harshly. 'I'm beginning to wonder what you've heard about mine. Let's call the past quits, shall we, and start from here—you and me, here and now.'

'All right.'

'Supposing ...' he said deliberately, 'I told you that I'm serious,' His voice sounded steady and almost casual. 'About you,' he added.

She looked up at him, startled. But his face gave her no clue. It was deliberately expressionless, watching for her reaction. Afraid to believe him, and made more sceptical by that watchful look, as though he was conducting an experiment, getting ready to note how she responded, she managed a cool little, disbelieving laugh. 'Serious?' she said. 'I wouldn't believe you.'

'Would you believe that I love you, Vanessa Morris? That I've wanted you ever since Bret used to bring you round to our place at the weekends? That if he hadn't been my brother I would have cut him out two years ago?'

Surprised and still wary, Vanessa took refuge in a flippant challenge.

'What makes you think you could have?' she asked.

She should have known how Thad would react to that. She tried to back away from him, but his arms allowed her no escape, and his mouth on hers demanded a sensual surrender, a tacit admission that she was less indifferent than she pretended. And when she submitted finally and gave him the response he was seeking, he whispered against her throbbing mouth, 'I love you.'

But Ross had said he loved her, once. All Vanessa's caution returned and she struggled free of his arms and moved away from him, leaving him angry and baffled as she asked him to drive her home.

It was not until Thad asked her to marry him that she finally dared to believe that his love was genuine, something more than transient desire. She confessed to him the reason for her hesitancy in accepting that he was sincere, and was grateful for an understanding she had been afraid to expect from him. In the days of their engagement she gave him every response he asked, and was conscious that her own love was deepened by his self-imposed limitation on what he demanded of her. If she needed it, his restraint was the final proof of his love for her. Their honeymoon had been all she believed a honeymoon should be, and her burgeoning love for her new husband had been heightened by a sense of gratitude for his unexpected sensitivity to her uncertainties and her need to feel respected as well as loved.

CHAPTER SEVEN

CLEMENTINA took some of Thad's figures and a few weeks later was asking for more. There were queries from two more shops as well, and Thad's future seemed assured. He was now making a modest but erratic income from sales. Celine was quite a frequent visitor, and sometimes when Vanessa arrived home from work she would be in the workroom with Thad, and she would hear the two of them laughing and talking together as she entered the house. Because she liked Celine as a person, it took a long time for Vanessa to admit to herself that she was jealous of the girl —jealous of her easy comradeship with Thad, of her ability to make him often laugh. That was a quality that had disappeared from her own relationship with her husband.

The weather had been turning cooler lately and Vanessa was more willing to accept Ross's offers of a ride home after work. It seemed silly to walk in pouring rain or a sharp cold wind when the journey, short as it was, could be accomplished in five minutes in a comfortable car. Usually he didn't try to detain her, but once when it was raining heavily she stayed in his car a few minutes waiting for the downpour to ease. She noticed him glancing at her almost covertly, as though he was wanting to ask her something, or expected something of her.

Vanessa looked back at him enquiringly, and he smiled. 'How is Thad?'

'Well,' she said. 'He's earning a living, now, with his work.' Lightly she added, 'I may be able to leave my job and turn to being a full-time housewife.'

At that moment a flash of lightning illuminated the car, and in the brief glare she caught a murderous look on Ross's face. But as distant thunder growled, she decided it must have been a trick of the atmospheric conditions. He looked perfectly normal as he said, 'I hope not, Vanessa. I wouldn't like to lose you.'

'That's flattering,' said Vanessa. 'But I don't think I want to spend my life working in a bank.'

'Why not?' he asked, and there was no mistaking the anger in his voice. '*I* do.'

Puzzled by his vehemence, she replied, 'Yes—but for you it's a career, not just a job behind the counter. I'm sorry if I offended you, Ross.'

Again he smiled, taking her hand briefly and taking it to his lips. 'I shouldn't have snapped at you, darling. Forgive me.'

Hastily she removed her hand from his grasp. As she turned to find the handle of the door he said, 'I still want you, you know.'

Involuntarily she turned her head to look at him. And it was true. She could see it in his eyes—desire and something else, something that made her uneasy. It looked almost like accusation.

'You—mustn't!' she protested. 'I'm married!'

'*Happily?*' He whipped out the question like a Gestapo interrogator, and afterwards she blamed herself bitterly for the momentary hesitation that ensued before she said, too loudly, 'Of course!'

'Of course!' he repeated sarcastically, with triumph glittering in his blue eyes. 'You make a very loyal little wife, Vanessa, but scarcely a happy one. Do you think I haven't noticed?'

'You're quite wrong,' she said weakly.

'Oh, no. No, I'm not wrong, Vanessa. But you always were a stubborn little—cuss. Why don't you admit the truth, and get out? Leave him—and come to me.'

She stared for a moment in shock. Then slowly she said, 'Ross—Thad is my husband and I love him. And even if I ever did leave him, you must understand that I would never come to you. Never.'

In a savage undertone, he said, 'You little fool!' His face frightened her.

'I'm sorry,' she whispered.

'*Sorry!*' He seemed to be controlling himself with some effort. 'One day you may well be!'

She opened the door and stumbled out, unheeding of the rain, and he drove off immediately, the tires throwing up jets of water in their wake.

In something like panic Vanessa raced inside the house, intent on telling Thad that she was going to leave her job. She couldn't stay at the bank any longer, now that Ross had revealed the unexpected persistence and depth of his desire for her. Always before she had regarded her continuing attraction for him as a shallow fancy, something that was partly a product of his own susceptibility to any good-looking woman, and partly of his pique at her terminating their earlier affair before he had tired of it himself. But now a dark undercurrent had surfaced and it frightened her. It frightened her more than the episode at Christmas, when he had been drinking quite heavily, and she was able to put down his behaviour to that. This time he had been quite sober.

She slipped off her wet shoes hastily at the door, but didn't bother to remove her coat before she hurried down the passageway to Thad's workroom. Celine was there.

She saw Celine first, and was hit by a sudden wave of frustrated anger, before she noticed that besides Thad, another man was in the room. A big man with a beard. Ritchie, of course, Celine's husband. Vanessa pushed wet hair out of her eyes and automatically acknowledged the introduction that Celine made, and was suddenly conscious of her damp and bedraggled appearance.

Thad said, 'You'd better go and change, Vanessa,' and she excused herself, wondering if he was ashamed of her before his friends.

Celine and her husband stayed for drinks, declining to have a meal and when they had gone Thad tossed her the mail that had come that day.

'There was an enormous repair bill for the car,' he told her. 'And our electricity bill gets bigger every month.'

The car had been giving trouble since Thad had been home, and the garage had worked on it for a whole day locating and fixing the problem. Vanessa's heart sank. If she left her job, they would be struggling to make ends meet.

She had a letter from a friend in Australia, and there were a couple of circulars. About to open the last envelope, she said, 'This one is for you, Thad, isn't it?'

The address was typewritten on the envelope, and he looked and said, 'Yes, it is. I must have put it in the wrong pile by mistake,' and took it from her.

He hesitated a moment before opening it, staring thoughtfully at the envelope, then he tore it open. He took out a single flimsy sheet of paper, glanced at it, said, 'Excuse me,' and went out of the room.

He had looked grim, his mouth slightly contorted, and Vanessa stared after him, puzzled by his manner. After a while she got slowly to her feet and followed him into the bedroom. He was standing at the window, staring out into the rain, his hands thrust into his pockets. When she entered the room he didn't move.

'Is anything wrong?' she asked.

He didn't answer, but after a few moments he turned to look at her. The room was gloomy, the day outside still wet and darkening early.

'Did Bray bring you home?' he asked abruptly.

'Yes.' She couldn't help recalling the conversation with Ross, then, and embarrassment coloured her cheeks. 'It was raining,' she said. 'Quite heavily.'

'I have offered to come and pick you up when it's wet,' he reminded her.

'I know. But there's a gas shortage, and it isn't far to walk.'

'But you didn't walk.'

'No, but—— Look, if you don't want me to let Ross give me a lift, I'll promise——'

'Keep your promises!' Thad interrupted harshly. 'Do what you like.'

He turned abruptly back to the window and the grey rain outside. He sounded as though he really didn't care what she did, and she didn't know what to do next. She had almost told him she was accepting no more rides from Ross anyway. But the rigidly rejecting back he had turned to her invited no confidences. She would have liked to tell him that Ross scared her, but she didn't know how to start. The last time she had tried to talk about Ross, Thad had accused her of trying to make him jealous. He didn't look as though he would be any more understanding this time.

Defeated, she turned away and returned to the other room.

*

In the morning the rain had disappeared, and the world looked freshly washed. The houhere outside their bedroom window had lost most of its dainty white flowers, that lay in a muddied carpet about its feet, but the dark green serrated leaves looked glossy with the wet. The rain had battered a few of the flowers in the garden, but what remained looked more alive and healthy than before, sparkling and nodding in the morning sunshine. And the intensity of Vanessa's encounter with Ross the day before began to fade in her memory; perhaps her imagination had supplied more drama than had been there, aided by the oppressive atmosphere of the rain and the thunder in the air.

The impression was strengthened by Ross's wholly normal greeting to her when he came into the bank. His quick glance over her green woollen dress and high-heeled shoes held mild admiration and nothing more, his smile was as warm as ever.

Last night he had told her that he still wanted her. But that meant no more to him than a passing compliment. He was still unmarried, and his position at the bank demanded a certain amount of discretion in a small town. Her presence occasionally tantalised him, she supposed, but any attractive woman might do the same. Certainly he treated them all to the same appreciative masculine appraisal that he had bestowed on her this morning. And no doubt on his frequent weekends away he found ample compensation for his circumspect behaviour during the week. She didn't believe for a moment that he had become less eager for female company—merely more discreet.

There was a small courtyard at the rear of the bank where on fine days the staff could sit on slatted benches and eat their lunch. There was a tub of variegated yellow and green coprosma spilling over the concrete flagstones, and a young kowhai tree allowed the sunshine to filter through its fern-like leaves. In spring it had been covered with a load of drooping, elongated blossoms weighing down the slender branches, but now only one or two faded blooms clung stubbornly among the foliage.

Vanessa had eaten her one sandwich and emptied a pot of fruit-flavoured yoghurt and was flipping through a magazine when the low-toned conversation of two of the male clerks penetrated her consciousness. They were sitting just along the seat from her, and although she tried to concentrate on the magazine, her eyes following carefully the list of ingredients for the mouth-watering tamarillo pie illustrated on the facing page, the men's words carried in spite of their lowered voices. They were talking about Ross. It was his name that had caught her ear.

'I suppose he is young for the job,' one was saying now. 'But he got it over the heads of older men. He must have impressed the bosses in Wellington, somehow.'

'Old Carpenter thought the job was his, you know.'

'Yes, well, I suppose it was a blow to be passed over. We all thought he'd get the job, as I recall. There was some feeling at the time that he'd been unfairly treated. Of course, he resigned soon after Bray was appointed.'

'Left town, too.'

'Yes. Mind you, I believe that soon after he resigned, there was a rather nasty implication made about him—some rumour floating round the town.'

'That he was too kind to young girls, you mean?' The man was whispering, but in a penetrating hiss. Vanessa hastily stood up, but she knocked over the flimsy yoghurt container, sending it rolling under her seat, and as she bent to retrieve it the conversation continued.

'You heard that, too?' asked the first man. 'Well, perhaps the disappointment had affected his mind a bit. And he had time on his hands, having retired early because of it.'

'Well, I don't know. *I* heard it had been going on for some time, in fact the reason he was passed over was because someone sent an anonymous letter to Head Office.'

'Would they take notice of that?'

As Vanessa straightened and walked away, she heard the soft ruminative reply. 'I don't know—no smoke without fire, perhaps ...'

The unwitting eavesdropping left a nasty taste, Vanessa found. Men, she thought, were worse gossips than women. She felt sorry for poor old Mr Carpenter whom she vaguely remembered as a small, bespectacled man with thinning grey hair who had worked at the bank for many years. How beastly if he had been driven away from the town where he had lived for so long because of a lot of vicious gossip, very likely with no foundation at all. She dropped her yoghurt carton in to the wastebasket by her desk and flung the magazine crossly on to the desk's surface. It was still open at the pie recipe. They had a tamarillo tree in the garden. She loved the dark red oval fruit, split open and with sugar sprinkled on the yellow and red flesh with its dark seeds. Her mother still called them tree tomatoes, scorning the 'fancy' name under which they were exported as a 'made-up label for foreigners'. The pie looked superb, with a meringue topping that would help to sweeten the tart flavour of the fruit. One of these days she would make it. She must remember to cut out the recipe.

Determinedly concentrating on other things, she managed to push the lunchtime conversation to the back of her mind. She hadn't been meant to overhear, although certainly it had not been her fault the two men failed to keep their voices sufficiently down. She had obviously been sitting only a few feet from them, after all. Anyway, she told herself, it could do her no good to remember it. She set herself to forget the episode as far as possible.

Celine had invited Thad and Vanessa to a barbecue party she was holding at the farm where her cottage was. While her husband was home she wanted to bring together some of their friends, to celebrate their third wedding anniversary.

The setting for the party was perfect. Not far from the house a small stream that began in the hills behind the farm widened into a natural pool, deep enough for swimming. Flat grey rock gave way to sheep-shorn grass on one bank, and native bush covered the other, dipping ferns into the stream as it trickled out through a narrow groove into small falls and rapids splashing over rounded grey stones. Further upstream the bush closed in on both sides of the stream, tall kahikateas and totaras pushing up through the tangle of punga, king ferns, manuka and red-tinged ladder-ferns that grew about the feet of their more stately neighbours.

Two portable barbecues were set up on the grass, and thirty or forty people took possession of the pool and its surrounds, disturbing a brilliant blue and cream kingfisher which flew with an indignant flurry of wings only a foot or so above their heads from his perch on a branch overhanging the stream, to disappear into the bush.

Several people laughed in surprise, and Celine said, 'Isn't he beautiful?'

There were murmurs of agreement, and Ritchie said, 'Did you know the Australian kookaburra is a member of the kingfisher family?'

'*No!*' Celine rounded mouth and eyes in exaggerated

astonishment. 'Thank you for that bit of useless information, Ritchie.'

Ritchie grinned and aimed a mock-blow at her while Celine squealed and ducked, giggling. They seemed supremely happy together, and Vanessa was ashamed of her occasional feelings of jealousy. She envied them their obvious happiness.

The barbecue fires were lit, and then the men and the women went off in different directions to don swimwear, except for those who had worn theirs under their clothes. Vanessa and Thad both swam, but not close to each other. Floating gently against the rocks in one corner, Vanessa covertly watched Thad's slow powerful crawl the length of the pool, and shivered with remembered sensations as she recalled the first time they had swum together after his return from the hospital, and its outcome.

Unaccountably, tears stung her eyes, and she turned away from the thronged pool to stare into the bush behind. It was green and mysterious, and she concentrated fiercely on the black-furred tightly curled heart of a small punga just within her vision, the spiral of fleshy embryonic growth that would soon unfurl itself into a long, graceful branch with lacy leaves bending on either side. A small fantail, blue-green and with fragile-looking, delicate legs, flitted into her view, perching precariously on a brittle, thin manuka stem. It dipped and swayed, apparently unafraid of the human noise emanating from the pool close by, its bright eyes gleaming as it cocked its head first one way, then another, and the absurd fan of feathers which gave it its name alternately opening and closing as it balanced itself on the swaying perch.

Then someone surfaced with a splash from the water beside Vanessa, and the small intruder took fright and whirred away into the thickness of the trees.

Turning, Vanessa saw a tall, broad young man sweeping water-darkened fair hair back off a notably good-looking face.

'Hi!' the newcomer grinned. 'Great spot for a party, isn't it?'

Smiling back at him, Vanessa agreed that indeed it was.

He introduced himself as Bruce Harris, and she reciprocated with her name. Seeing a tattoo on his left forearm, she took a guess and said, 'Are you a sailor, like Ritchie?'

'Look like it, do I?' he grinned. 'Yes. We're on the same ship.'

It wasn't difficult to get him to talk about his travels, and he did so until he saw her shiver and exclaimed with remorse. 'Hell! I'm sorry, boring you with my life story, and here you are freezing to death.'

Laughing, she said, 'No, I'm not. I'm enjoying listening to you, but I think I will get moving for a while, and then get out. It *is* getting a bit chilly.'

The sun had set, and Ritchie, who had left the water and dressed, was lighting a couple of old-fashioned kerosene lamps while his wife unwrapped steak, sausages and lamb chops for the barbecue. Celine looked magnificent in a vivid caftan that skimmed her lush figure, with her red-gold hair pulled off her face with a blue satin ribbon, and allowed to cascade down her back.

Vanessa pulled on her fashion jeans and a light wool sweater in an oatmeal fleck, and strolled over to offer her help. Thad, who had left the pool just before she did, was helping to baste some steaks with a special sauce which Celine claimed was her own secret concoction. Vanessa was set to work uncovering the prepared salads and cole slaw and setting them out on a convenient flat rock, with baskets of delicious crusty home-made bread.

Bruce Harris materialised at her side. 'Feeling warmer now?' he asked.

'Yes, thank you,' Vanessa smiled. She folded the cloth that had been covering the last loaf of bread, and saw him eyeing her hands as she did so. She wondered if he had not noticed her wedding ring before, and if he would make some excuse now to wander off. He had only been ordinarily friendly, but now he had sought her out, and he was young and seemingly unattached. She thought she recalled seeing him arrive, and he had been alone. He might feel his time was wasted talking to a married woman.

But he sat down instead, perching on the edge of the rock she had just set the food on, and said, 'They're lucky with the weather, aren't they? After last week I thought summer was finished for good.'

'Yes, it has been cold lately. Thad—my husband, said Celine was crazy, thinking of a barbecue.'

'I reckon they're both crazy,' he grinned, looking briefly across at their host and hostess. 'But that's one of the nice things about them, don't you think?' Looking back at her, he added, 'Don't mind me saying that. Ritchie's a great mate of mine, you know. I suppose you're a friend of Celine's?'

'My husband is—well, we both are,' she added hastily, as his eyebrows rose a fraction. 'But I met her through Thad. They both do pottery.'

'I see.' He looked mildly thoughtful. His eyes wandered back to the barbecue area and the crowd. Following his gaze, she saw Celine, her hair gleaming in the light from the fire, put her hand on Thad's shoulder and lean close to say something to him that made him laugh.

'That's my husband, with Celine,' she said, pleased that

her voice sounded casual. It still hurt her that Celine could so often make Thad laugh spontaneously, while she herself seemed to have lost that power.

But Bruce's thoughtful gaze, returning to her, had a small gleam of speculation in it, she thought. Hastily she laughed lightly and said, 'You're sitting on the table, you know. Just as well this isn't a *hangi*!'

He moved and began to stroll back with her to the crowd. 'I don't get it, though,' he said. 'What's the difference between a barbecue and a *hangi*—except, of course that *hangi* food is cooked in pits in the ground?'

'Didn't you know that according to Maori etiquette, it's very bad manners to sit on a table used for food?'

'No, I didn't. Most *pakehas* are pretty ignorant of Maori customs, aren't they? Do you know a lot about it?'

'Not a lot. A little picked up from Maori friends, and some from books.'

Vanessa introduced Bruce to Thad, half expecting the other man to drift away, but he didn't. He spent a lot of the evening with them, even as groups broke up and re-formed, and when they had all eaten more than enough, and some dance records were put on the portable player that had been brought over from the house, he asked Vanessa to dance before Thad did.

On the grass it was only possible to do modern improvisational dancing, but Bruce was good at it, and a number of discs had been played before she said protestingly that she had had enough, and they returned to where Thad had been sitting. But he was gone, and was dancing with Celine, the girl's hair rippling with the reflected light from the kerosene lamps that hung from nearby branches, the curves under the clinging caftan emphasised by the sensuous undulations of her body. Ritchie was on the other side of the swaying dancers on the grass, with a plump, black-haired girl in too-tight trousers and an Indian blouse.

Bruce sat down close beside her, and when she made to move away he put a heavy arm about her shoulders and she felt his lips nuzzle her cheek. She wondered how much he had drunk of the red and white wines they had been served, or the hock that Ritchie had brought back with him from his last trip.

Decisively she pushed his arm away and moved, leaving a couple of feet between them.

'I thought you liked me,' said Bruce, sounding aggrieved.

'I do like you,' Vanessa replied. 'But you know quite well I'm married.'

'Thad's married, too. Doesn't seem to make much difference to *him*, does it? Is he a dog in the manger?'

'What on earth do you think you're talking about?' Vanessa asked coldly.

'Look, let's not get into an argument,' Bruce said placatingly. 'I'm sorry if I went too fast for you, but in my job there's often not much time. Heck, I only kissed your cheek, Vanessa. There's no reason to act like an outraged virgin. I thought maybe we could get together some time.'

'I told you,' she said emphatically, 'I'm *married*!'

'To Thad.' His eyes wandered meaningfully back to where Thad was dancing with Celine.

'Yes. To Thad.' Angrily she said, 'And for someone who's supposed to be a friend of Ritchie's, I think you're being pretty low to suggest that there's anything—anything *wrong* between his wife and my husband!'

Bruce looked at her frowningly, and then said slowly, 'I guess I got things wrong. Sorry—I thought you knew, you see. The way you didn't seem to mind your husband being so—affectionate with Celine.'

'You're jumping to a lot of conclusions,' Vanessa said hotly. 'Celine is an affectionate person. For heaven's sake, don't you think Ritchie would object if——'

She stopped at the sudden laugh that Bruce gave. 'Ritchie can't object!' he said. 'Didn't you know? When those two got married they solemnly promised not to curb each other's freedom—in *any* way! And Ritchie, at least, takes full advantage of the bargain, I can tell you!' Looking at her stunned face, he said more soberly, 'I'm sorry—I figured you and Thad had one of those modern arrangements, too. It looked like it, you see.'

Flatly, Vanessa said, 'Did it? Well, we don't.'

'Well,' he said uncomfortably, 'I daresay I was wrong about Thad.'

And Vanessa thought, *are you*? Aloud she said, 'Yes.'

'Look, Vanessa,' said Bruce, 'don't think too badly of me for making a mistake, will you? Or of Ritchie and Celine. They just didn't feel ready for marriage, you see—not for the whole bit, but they are in love, you can see that.'

'Yes, I see. And I can't understand——'

'Well, these days most people would have settled for just living together. They wanted something more, I guess. Some sort of commitment.'

Vanessa remembered Celine saying something of the sort. But she had not then realised the rest of it.

'It's their business,' she said. 'I expect they'll work it out, in the end.'

Their marriage was different from other people's in several ways. They spent a good deal of time apart, for one thing. And apparently they didn't feel that fidelity was a necessary part of the relationship.

And if Celine didn't feel bound by her marriage vows, would she be satisfied with only friendship from Thad, a man she saw quite often, who was easily as attractive as her husband, and would still be around when Ritchie had gone back to sea, and to what Vanessa could only suppose was the modern equivalent of the age-old sailor's 'girl in every port'.

Suspicion writhed snake-like inside her as she turned to see Celine coming over the grass, with Thad's arm about her waist, laughing up into his smiling face. If only she had been sure of his love for herself, and happily secure in it, the ugly thoughts would never have gained a toe-hold. But she knew that between her and Thad something was horribly wrong, that whatever he felt for her, it was not the emotion he had felt when they were first married, but something less than love.

CHAPTER EIGHT

THERE was a week-long craft exhibition held in Rotorua in April, and Celine persuaded Thad to exhibit some of his work. Lately he had been drawing some attention from fellow-craftsmen and the proprietor of a small gallery for clay sculpture with a highly glazed finish, as well as interestingly intricate plant holders and some large, chunky ceramic animals.

Vanessa had always liked Rotorua, and was glad when Thad suggested they should spend the weekend there, returning on Sunday night. They booked into one of the city's numerous motels, arriving there late on Friday night. Celine and Ritchie were staying in the same place, and on the Saturday morning the four of them went to the hall where the exhibition was being mounted, in convoy, with

Thad and Vanessa following the other car. Both cars held the exhibits they had brought, carefully packed in cartons. The day was overcast with small patches of blue sky occasionally glimpsed as the high clouds parted briefly. The lake looked a dull blue-grey colour, and the natural steam that arose here and there from the thermal activity around its shores looked more eerie than ever in the dull light. The pervading smell of sulphur that characterised Rotorua area faded a little as they entered the hall, each carefully carrying one of the boxes from their cars.

The place was already buzzing with activity, the long tables set out in rows and covered with cream cloth beginning to fill with the work of artists from all over the country. Celine and Thad were each allotted a space, and began to arrange their pieces to best advantage.

By lunchtime all was in readiness, and as the official opening was not until the following day, that left the afternoon free. They all lunched together in a city restaurant, and as they emerged the sun broke through drifting clouds and the day began to look considerably brighter.

'Mmm, that's better!' Celine exclaimed. 'Who fancies a boat trip to Mokoia?'

The Island, gently humped, rose blue and mysterious in the centre of the lake, its remoteness shrouded in legend.

'I'd like to,' Vanessa said. 'I've visited Rotorua several times, but never been on the lake.'

'Mokoia it is, then,' said Ritchie, glancing at Thad for confirmation and receiving an answering nod. 'We'll go and find one of those tourist launches.'

Although it was hardly the flush of the tourist season, the boat was quite full. Australian, American and European accents floated over the waters of the lake, and cameras clicked as visitors turned to get pictures of the city which had taken the name of the lake, with its scattered plumes and wisps of steam rising from among the buildings. The whole town had been built on an area of constant thermal activity, and even along the roadsides there were small stone cairns built to prevent the unwary from stepping into small fissures in the ground from which hissing steam escaped; and often if one listened, the boiling and bubbling of the earth's core could be heard.

Vanessa turned to watch the graceful island coming closer, as their guide retold the story of the legendary lovers, Hinemoa and Tutanekai. It was a Romeo and Juliet tale, of a girl and a man belonging to different, warring tribes. Hinemoa, the girl, lived on the shores of the lake, and Tutanekai on the island of Mokoia. They met on the shore and pledged their love, but the elders of Hinemoa's tribe would not allow her to marry her young lover. Sadly Tutanekai returned to his island home, but every night he would play his flute, the notes floating across the gentle waters of the lake to where Hinemoa sat on the far shore, grieving for her lost love.

One night, unable to bear the separation any longer, Hinemoa girdled herself with gourds to help keep her afloat, and entered the cold waters to swim to the island and Tutanekai. She was afraid, because the lake was inhabited by a fierce *taniwha*, a water monster, but her love was greater than fear, and eventually, cold and exhausted, she reached the island unharmed.

Eyeing the gap between the island and the lake shore as the boat nosed into the jetty, Ritchie grinned at Celine and asked, 'Would you swim that lake for me?'

'Not a chance!' she answered cheerfully. 'Especially if there was a *taniwha* lurking down there waiting to eat me up.'

She looked over the side of the launch, as Vanessa, smiling at their exchange, caught Thad's eyes on her. He wasn't smiling, but looking at her with a strange intensity. She thought, *I would have done it, for Thad.* The look deepened, and he took a step towards her, but Celine was saying, 'Oh, do look, you two. It's fantastic!'

Thad turned aside, and Vanessa joined him at the railing, looking down into water so clear that every stone on the bottom of the lake was visible, shining blue, grey, white, purple, through the slight ripples on the surface. A trout swam lazily near the boat, then flipped its tail and darted away until its brown speckled back merged with the shingle on the lake floor and it disappeared.

The passengers trooped ashore and were taken to the small hot spring where Hinemoa had warmed herself in the pool after her long swim. Here, in the morning, Tutanekai had discovered her, and had taken her to his house as his bride.

Later the tourists wandered in small groups all over the island, exploring the grassy flat near the shore, the bush-covered steeper slopes, and the shoreline with its overhanging pohutukawas. In summer the island was surrounded by a red wash of colour as the scarlet blossoms of the pohutukawa dropped into the lake.

Vanessa wasn't sure how they became separated from Celine and Ritchie, but as the afternoon drew on she and Thad found themselves alone, walking under the twisted, heavy branches of pohutukawas, glimpsing the lapping water of the lake through the leaves.

Thad said, 'Let's sit down,' and took her hand, guiding her to a grassy hollow formed by the humped-up arching of some huge grey roots, and virtually hidden by the heavy grey-green foliage that overhung it. Vanessa rested her back against one of the roots, and Thad stretched full-length on the grass.

She watched the gentle dipping and swaying of the branches, and the rippling of the lake glimpsed through them.

'It's very peaceful here,' she said. 'An island of love.'

'And war,' he reminded her. 'The reason Tutanekai's tribe chose to live here was the fact that it made a good stronghold. Life was cheap in those days.'

'Love wasn't.'

'No. Would *you* have risked your life for love, like Hinemoa?'

'You mean, for you?'

'All right—for me.'

'Of course I would. *You* did, for me.'

Thad's mouth gave a slightly twisted smile, but his eyes looked away. 'Oh, yes,' he said, 'I did.'

'Are you sorry?' she asked, perplexed.

His eyes blazed at her. 'Don't be bloody silly!'

Vanessa blinked and looked away.

Thad sat up, and she stiffened. In the small space he seemed very near. He said, on an odd note, 'Vanessa, do you believe that if a person saves your life, your life belongs thereafter to him?'

'I don't know,' she said, turning to look at him, trying to read the expression in his black eyes. 'But my life belonged to you, anyway.'

'And mine to you,' he said, his voice deep and husky. His hand reached out and touched her hair, stroking over it to the nape of her neck, then curving to bring her closer. She clutched at his shoulders to keep her balance as he tipped her face with both hands to look into her eyes.

'Tell me you love me,' he commanded. 'Say it.'

'I love you,' she whispered, just before he captured her mouth with his. Her lips parted under his insistent, sensuous demand, and as his hands moved and pulled her closer, her arms went around his neck. He pushed her back into the softness of the grass and his body pressed hers into it, while he kept kissing her with rising passion. Her hands moved over the hard muscles beneath his shirt, and his roamed over her body, gently arousing, until her desire matched his.

His fingers slid underneath her blouse to unhook her bra and tease her into a greater excitement, and then over the soft skin to her waist, pulling open the fastening of her jeans.

Vanessa stirred in protest, freeing her mouth to whisper, 'Oh, Thad! We can't—not here. What if someone comes——'

'I don't care a damn,' he muttered, his hand sliding to her hip while his mouth explored her throat and moved down to the warm swell of her breast. 'Do you?'

Feebly, she pushed momentarily against him, but the sweet heat of passion would not be denied. As his hold on her became even more intimate she capitulated, saying softly, 'No ... no. I don't care ...'

They scrambled back on the boat with only minutes to spare, but as they were not the only ones their lateness was not conspicuous.

Later they wandered around the Maori village of Ohinemutu, contemplating the unique bust of Queen Victoria surmounting a platform carved in the intricate fashion of Maori art; and visiting the tiny church where the sandblasted picture of a Maori Christ in feather cloak 'walked' on the water of the lake as seen through the big window on which it was etched.

They wandered in the grounds of the government gardens, where the rosebeds and specimen trees were dominated by the huge old mock-Tudor building which had once been the bath-house and was now converted into a restaurant and reception rooms. Here, too, hot pools were bounded by stone walls, and near the lake's edge steam oozed gently from cracks in the whitened ground, and streaks of yellow sulphur added a touch of colour.

They returned to the motel with takeaway hamburgers and cartoned ice-cream sundaes, and then Celine and Ritchie suggested a swim at the blue baths in the government gardens.

Thad smiled across at Vanessa lazily, in a way she didn't remember his having done for a long time. 'Are you game?' he asked.

'It's warmer than the lake,' she said.

He threw back his head and laughed, and she felt a surge of happiness. There had been a different, more gentle quality in his lovemaking on the island this afternoon, and in his arm about her waist, his hand firmly holding hers in their later wanderings. Perhaps things at last were coming right.

The blue baths were smartly tiled and very civilised, with a big pool for swimming and a smaller one with a series of diving boards, but the water was natural mineral water, pumped from the boiling springs outside the building, and cooled just enough for comfort. The swimming was pleasant but enervating. After an hour or so they left the water feeling deliciously drowsy.

'I could sleep for a week,' Celine said as they climbed into her car.

'You'd miss the exhibition,' her husband grinned as he started the engine. 'What a waste!'

'Wouldn't care,' Celine sighed, leaning her head on his shoulder.

In the back seat, Thad quietly slid his arm about Vanessa to allow her to follow suit. After a momentary hesitation she did, and was blissfully contented when she felt his lips brush against her temple. The ride back to the motel was all too short, and she was reluctant to leave Thad's encircling arm for the cool night air. When he turned on the light in their room she blinked at its harshness, and he laughed and said, 'You're half asleep already. Go to bed.' His hands turned her gently in the direction of the bedroom, and she kicked off her shoes sleepily and sat on the bed.

Minutes later when he came in from the bathroom, she was still there, and he came over to her and over her sleepy protests helped her to undress and put on her nightgown.

He came into the bed beside her and she let her head rest on his chest where she could hear his beating heart. For the first time since their honeymoon, she slept in his arms.

Judging by the crowd who arrived on the first day, the exhibition was going to be a roaring success. Several people showed interest in Thad's exhibits on the Sunday morning, and he was hopeful of some orders before the week was out. Celine was staying for the entire week, and had promised to look after Thad's interests as well as her own when he had gonc home.

They had sandwiches for lunch, snatched quickly before returning to the exhibition hall, and at about three-thirty, Thad found Vanessa sitting in a corner, her head leaning against the wall behind her. She straightened as she watched him approach, and smiled, but the concerned look in his eyes didn't fade.

'What's the trouble?' he asked. 'Had enough?'

'It's all right—I'm fine,' she said. He had been deep in conversation with a wood-carver, and she knew he was finding the day stimulating, whereas she had already viewed all the displays at least twice, and the noise and the tobacco smoke in the air had given her a headache. 'I'll go and take a short walk in the fresh air,' she said, standing up.

Thad took her arm in a firm grip and said, 'We both will, and then we'll go home.'

'I'm sure you don't want to go yet——'

'Don't argue. How do you know what I want, anyway?'

He steered her through the crowd and in no time they had said goodbye to Celine and Ritchie, and were outside on the street.

On the way to the car they passed a souvenir shop, open for the tourist trade. The small window was jammed full of carved wooden boxes and multi-coloured paua shell trinkets, greenstone *tikis* and their cheap plastic imitations, and leatherwork featuring the spiral designs typical of Maori art.

Thad stopped and steered her into the narrow shop. 'I'll buy you a souvenir,' he said.

He settled on a tiny paua shell *tiki* suspended from a fine silver chain. The grotesque little figure, three-fingered hands folded in front of its squat body, its head on one side and with a long pointed tongue protruding, was certainly not beautiful in itself, but the iridescent shell gave it a certain charm. And the significance of the *tiki* to the Maori in ensuring good fortune and warding off evil was well known to *pakeha* New Zealanders as well; the inexpensive little gift pleased Vanessa greatly.

They returned to the car, and Thad asked, 'Would you like to take a short walk around Whakarewarewa before we go home?'

They drove to the southern end of the town and crossed the bridge where Maori children traditionally dived into the stream for the tourists' coins, to enter the scenic attraction. The path took them past a row of houses where some of the housewives still cooked their meals by lowering a basket of food into a convenient boiling pool at the back door, and natural hot baths were located in several of the back yards. Then it went uphill, bordered by a picket fence decorated with hand-carved figures, and led them to the area of intense thermal activity that made 'Whaka' famous. Boiling water spurted from rumbling holes at their feet, and the surface of the white rock was dusted with bright yellow sulphur.

Warm streams and cold ones ran side by side, and boiling mud bubbled like porridge, or in the pool known as the 'frog pond', leaped and plopped like frogs jumping.

'That's always been one of my favourites,' Vanessa confessed, as they laughed over it, leaning on the railing that prevented the tourists from joining the activity below.

Thad smiled down at her and gently touched her cheek with his hand before he took hers and led her away to the path. Rather than make the long uphill climb to the model Maori village and the carvers' school, which they would not have time to visit, they retraced their steps the way they had come, gaining a good view of the pretty little bridal veil falls, and being further rewarded by the eruption of the spectacular Pohutu geyser.

As the ground trembled under their feet, and a premonitory rumble announced the geyser's imminent appearance, Thad's arm tightened about Vanessa's waist. Then with a tremendous, continuous roar, a plume of hot water thrust into the air, more than twenty feet high, the steam billowing into the atmosphere and sending warm droplets like fine rain on to their faces. They stood fascinated, close together, until the rocks about the geyser were awash with water, and the sound and fury had abated a little, the plume of water dropping back, starting up again, then dropping further.

'I've never seen it perform so well,' Vanessa said, almost awestruck.

'We've been lucky, this trip,' said Thad.

'Oh, yes,' she agreed, 'we've been lucky.' But she meant it in more ways than one.

On Thursday evening Thad's parents celebrated their fortieth wedding anniversary. It was one of the reasons Thad had decided not to stay in Rotorua for the week, because the family was to gather at the homestead for the occasion.

Vanessa had a new dress for the party, and was planning to wash her hair after work, using her small blow-dryer and a curling iron to effect a pretty new style for her hair. So she was exasperated when at the end of the bank's day, an error in accounting had to be discovered and corrected to ascertain that some money had not actually gone missing. The extra time made her late, and when Ross offered to drive her home she accepted after only a momentary hesitation, in spite of her previous resolutions not to accept any more lifts from him.

Her relationship with Thad over the last few days had been so much better that she no longer feared that he would be difficult if he noticed that Ross had brought her home, and the uneasy memory of her last encounter with Ross in the privacy of his car had faded.

The uneasiness stirred again, however, when he said, as he swung round the corner into her street, 'I'm tempted to keep driving, Vanessa, and take you home with me.'

'I'm going out tonight,' she said lightly. 'You wouldn't want to make me late.'

'Wouldn't I?' he murmured. She remembered that low, sexy note in his voice from the days when she had foolishly imagined herself in love with him, and the memory almost made her smile with self-derision. 'What would you say,' he went on in the same tone, 'if I asked you to come home with me one day? You'd like my house. It's very—private.'

'I'd say no,' she said crisply.

He said nothing for a few moments, drawing up outside her door and turning off the engine.

She reached for the handle of the door. But he caught at her wrist and held it, taking her other hand, too, in his. Vanessa pulled away, without effect except to make him tighten his grip.

He said, 'I meant what I said, Vanessa. Remember last time we talked?' His eyes strayed hotly over her face and figure. 'I'm obsessed with you—I want you so much. Vanessa, I love you, darling.'

'Ross, stop it! I told you, *I love Thad*!'

'As much as you once loved *me*? Didn't you mean it when you said you loved me?'

'That was a long time ago, Ross. I was too young to know what love meant.'

'Until I taught you!'

His arrogance was breathtaking. Disliking him intensely, she snapped angrily, 'Whatever you taught me, Ross, it wasn't how to love. You didn't know how to do that. I doubt if you do now!'

'*Damn you!* I'll teach you one lesson you'll never forget!' he said furiously, and dragged her into his arms, holding her in a grip that hurt while he savaged her mouth with his.

Her struggles were useless against his strength in the confined space of the car, and the more she fought the more he hurt her. It was less a kiss than an attack, and she began to feel frightened. Never had she imagined that his feelings —whatever they were—went as deep as this.

She stopped trying to escape and concentrated on enduring his hot mouth on hers, his hurting hands. Then he tried to coax her, with little sensual tricks that she remembered, but that now left her cold as ice in his arms. As soon as they relaxed their grip a little, she pulled fiercely away. Again he grabbed her wrists, and she said icily, 'Let me go, Ross. I couldn't bear to touch you—in any way! I won't hit you.'

'Don't pretend,' he said, and she almost gasped aloud at the depth of his self-deception, his arrogance. It was useless talking to him.

This time he didn't try to stop her when she found the door handle and got out.

The last few days, Thad had greeted her with a smile and a kiss when she came home, but today when she pushed open the door of his workroom he was sitting with his back to her, his hands smoothing and shaping a large piece of clay, its grey surface shiny and smooth, rounded contours beginning to form from a shapeless mass. His fingers pushed strongly at the clay.

She would have gone over to him, leaning on his shoulders to drop a light kiss on his cheek, but the episode she had just gone through had disturbed her, and although she had not welcomed Ross's lovemaking, something held her back from going straight to her husband from his arms. She stood in the doorway and said, 'Hello, I'm home.'

He didn't look round from what he was doing. 'Hello,' he said.

'You're very busy.'

'I'm trying to get this done—the basic shape anyway—before we go out.' He glanced around at her then, and for a second or two his eyes seemed to rest on her mouth. It throbbed with the aftermath of Ross's cruelty, and she was aware of a taste of blood against her tongue. Suddenly alarmed, she wondered if it showed—what had happened.

But Thad had turned indifferently back to his work. 'Would you mind fixing me something I can eat in here?' he asked.

'All right,' she said. 'I suppose a snack will do? Knowing your mother she'll have prepared a feast for tonight.'

'Yes,' he said absently, 'I expect she will have.'

In the mirror, Vanessa could see that her lipstick was gone, but otherwise her face looked quite normal, if a little pale. She would use some blusher tonight to correct that. She supposed that tomorrow she had better hand in her resignation. She decided to do it first and tell Thad afterwards. She supposed she would have to tell him the reason—in his present mood he would no doubt understand. But tonight he was preoccupied, and then there was the party. She sighed, and went to the kitchen to prepare some food.

When she put his filled bread roll and cup of coffee on a clear space of the old pine table he hardly glanced at her, his fingers busy shaping the clay, that had already begun to vaguely resemble a reclining human form.

'What is it going to be?' she asked, and his fingers suddenly curled and slipped over the clay, making a raking mark that even she could see was a bad mistake.

Thad cursed under his breath, and she said, 'I'm sorry, I didn't mean to spoil your concentration.'

He threw a look at her that surprised her by its obvious fury, and she quickly murmured another apology and left the room. Thad was developing an artistic temperament, she decided wryly. She would have to watch herself when he was working, that was obvious.

The party was as noisy and gay as the Nelson family gatherings always were. Other friends and neighbours were there, too, and every room was crowded. Vanessa soon found herself separated from Thad, and, determined to erase the uncomfortable feeling left by her confrontation with Ross, she set out to enjoy herself. Things were already in full swing when they arrived, because she had taken some time to fix her hair, and Thad had not emerged and begun to dress for ages, leaving them with little time to cover the few miles to the Nelson farm.

She danced on the minute cleared space improvised for the purpose in the dining room, with Owen, Thad's brother-in-law, while Nicola was putting the baby to bed. Then she played for a while with the irrepressible Sara, Thad's niece, who was allowed to stay up late on this occasion.

She had danced a few more times before supper, with Bret once, and Sara's father, Ken, and then with others. She glimpsed Thad once or twice, the first time dancing with Clem, who was looking particularly striking tonight in a pale blue, cunningly cut sheath of her own design.

'I love that dress,' Vanessa told the other girl sincerely,

when they both sank down on a sofa after a particularly energetic dance. Bret had offered to get them both a drink.

'Thank you. I like yours, too. That rose colour suits you beautifully. And I like the new hairstyle, too. I don't know why Thad isn't glued to your side.'

'I'll second that,' said Bret, appearing out of the crowd with a tall glass in each hand. 'Gin and lime for you, Vanessa, and Pimms for Clementina.' He handed over the glasses and added, 'Taking a risk, isn't he, that husband of yours—leaving you to the mercy of this lot?' He glanced teasingly around the room.

'I'm enjoying myself,' she smiled. 'I expect he is, too. Some of these people haven't seen him since he left the hospital.'

Brent looked rather thoughtful. 'As you say, he seems to be enjoying himself.'

A child's cry of protest made them turn to see little Sara struggling in her mother's arms as Elaine tried to carry her out of the room. 'Auntie 'nessa!' the child cried. 'I want Auntie 'nessa to put me to bed.'

Vanessa rose immediately and crossed the room to Elaine's side.

'May I?' she asked. 'I don't mind.'

Elaine relinquished her hold on the little girl, who was struggling to transfer her small body into Vanessa's arms. 'I shouldn't give in to her, really, she's being very naughty. But she is overtired. Thank you, Vanessa.' As her daughter wound her arms tightly about Vanessa's neck, pointedly turning her face from her mother, she added, 'I'm not popular at the moment, obviously!'

'Where do I put her?' Vanessa asked.

'In Nicola's old room. It's reasonably quiet, and the bed is made up.'

Sara insisted on a story, and Vanessa settled on *The Sleeping Beauty* in the hope that the power of suggestion might be at work. The bright eyes in the small face were still open when she had finished, but a soft-voiced lullaby soon closed them, and the child slept.

Vanessa stayed a few more minutes to be sure, and then got up to tiptoe to the door. A tall shadow loomed in the doorway, and she thought it was Thad, and sped across the room eagerly, only to stop short when she recognised Bret's deep voice saying, 'Supper is served. I volunteered to come and get you before it's all gone. Is she asleep?'

'Yes,' she said softly. 'Like an angel. Thanks for coming to get me, Bret.'

She stepped out into the passageway, but as she made to pass him he touched her arm and stopped her.

'Have you and Thad had a row?' he asked.

'No. Why should you think that?'

'It isn't like him to drink as much as he's been doing to-night. Are things still difficult between you?'

'No,' she assured him. 'Things are much better. We're happy—truly.'

'I'm glad,' he said. 'Perhaps he's celebrating—although I must say that if it were me, I'd be celebrating by staying close by my beautiful wife.'

Smiling, she said, 'Now, I don't know if that means me or Clem.'

Bret grinned. 'You're both very beautiful women, in entirely different ways. And I love you both——'

'In entirely different ways!' she added for him.

'Are you sure things are all right?' he asked, looking at her searchingly.

'Yes,' she said, suppressing a small, nagging doubt that had been deliberately hidden over the last few days—a doubt because Thad had insisted, that day on Mokoia, that she declared her love, but he had not put his own feelings into words.

'Good,' he said, and putting his hands briefly on her shoulders, he kissed her forehead.

'That's *my wife* you're kissing!' Thad's hard voice snapped from the passage doorway.

As Bret's hands dropped, and Vanessa turned in surprise, Thad pulled closed the door behind him with a sharp click. The noise of the party became a muffled background blur, and the passageway suddenly seemed very narrow and confining as Thad's black eyes challenged Bret over Vanessa's head.

Easily, Bret said, 'Tit for tat, Thad. I seem to remember on one occasion I came on you kissing Clementina in this very house. It was an equally innocent kiss, of course.'

'Innocent,' agreed Thad, and then he laughed briefly, softly. 'Well, Clem was innocent, anyway. She wasn't, at the time, married to you, was she?'

'No. We were engaged. She was wearing my ring.'

'Rings,' said Thad, 'don't mean much to some women. Even wedding rings.'

'That is not a charge that can be levelled at my wife—or yours.' Bret's voice was still quiet, but there was unmistakably a thread of steel running through it.

Driven by some instinct, Vanessa moved aside a little, coming up against the wall. The two men, equally tall, both emanating a virile strength, faced each other in a clash of two strong wills. Bret's cool grey eyes were wary and implacable, Thad's dark ones glittered with angry challenge.

Appalled, she glanced from one brother to the other. Thad was unmistakably spoiling for a fight, and Bret, while he would avoid it, if he could, was not a man to allow himself—or especially Clem—to be insulted, even by his own brother. His mouth was grim, and Thad's was twisted into a faint, bitter smile.

Then behind him the door opened, and Elaine came through, breaking the awful tension.

'Is the little horror asleep yet?' she asked Vanessa, apparently quite unaware of any intrusion.

'Yes,' answered Vanessa, on a long pent-up breath. 'She's fine, Elaine.' As though released from a spell, she moved towards Thad, touching him, and saying, 'I'm hungry—let's go and get some of your mother's delicious supper.'

He put up his hands and held her arms in a grip that hurt, and for a moment she thought he was going to thrust her aside. Then he removed one of his hands and turned her to go through the doorway, as Elaine passed on her way to check her daughter.

He said, 'Sure, let's join the party ... I've scarcely seen you all night, and you're worth seeing tonight, my darling. The dress is——' his eyes roved over her bare shoulders, down to the vee that dipped between her breasts, and the soft moulding of the material over her hips, '—very sexy,' he finished. He smiled down at her, but his eyes had a cruel glitter in their depths, and his hand on her arm was painful as he steered her into the room.

For the rest of the evening, he did stay by her side, but his mood seemed to be one of coiled watchfulness that became almost oppressive. Vanessa scarcely tasted the succulent white crayfish flesh that was a rare treat these days, nestling in crisp lettuce leaves on the table, and Mrs Nelson's mouthwatering pavlova, its light and fluffy meringue base topped with fresh whipped cream and rings of green, juicy kiwi-fruit, might have been cardboard for all it meant to her.

She had been shocked and worried by the near flare-up in the passage. It had been ridiculous for Thad to be jealous of Bret, but then he always had been, a little, and perhaps the fact that, as Bret said, he had been drinking more than usual might have made him prone to exaggerate that trivial incident of Bret's fleeting kiss.

He didn't seem drunk at all, only the glitter of his eyes and a hardly noticeable deliberate clarity in speech giving any sign. That, and the slight but unmistakable sarcasm he used when he spoke to her.

'My brother thinks I've been neglecting you,' he murmured, as he pulled her into his arms on the dance floor, after the food had been cleared away. 'Were you complaining to him?'

'Of course not!' Vanessa tipped back her head to look at him. 'I told him I was enjoying myself, and so were you.'

'Did you indeed? Always the loyal little wife, aren't you?'

His grip tightened suddenly on her waist, the fingers digging into her flesh through the thin fabric of her dress.

'Thad, *don't*! You're hurting me!'

'Am I?' He sounded savage, as though he didn't care, or perhaps *wanted* to hurt her, but his grip relaxed a little and he danced in silence after that.

A stirring of anger mingled with hurt in Vanessa's emotions. Already, today, Ross had manhandled her—her inner lip still throbbed with a small swelling from his brutal kiss, and her arm tingled where he had held her to stop her struggling—and now Thad seemed determined to treat her equally roughly.

The party ceased to be a pleasure and became an ordeal. She dared not suggest they leave early, because she wanted to ensure that the evening was a happy one for Thad's parents, and an early departure would have them wondering what was wrong. Besides, the way Thad was acting, it would be like him to prolong the agony, just because he thought she wanted to terminate it ...

She caught Bret's narrowed gaze on them once or twice, but no one else appeared to notice anything amiss. She was relieved that Bret did not again come near them, because she was sure that trouble would have ensued if he had.

At last people began to drift away, and Vanessa, still gallantly smiling and doing her best to give the impression she was having a great time, could hope that the long evening was nearly over.

When Thad said in her ear, 'Do you want to go home?' she drooped against him a little with sheer relief.

'Yes,' she said. 'Please.'

On the journey home she sat tensely beside him as he drove in total silence, only slowing for an occasional opossum that was caught in the glare of the headlights before loping off the road into the darkness. When he had garaged the car she got out without waiting for him, but by the time she reached the door he was with her. She would have had to wait, anyway, because he had brought his key, and she had not hers with her. He stood close to her, trying to find the lock in the darkness. Warmth emanated from his body, and the faint smell of the drink he had been imbibing at the party.

The door swung open, and he stood aside for her to brush by him. Vanessa fumbled for the light switch, and closed her eyes against the sudden glare as she heard the door click behind her.

Thad's hand removed the light wool wrap that covered her shoulders, then he turned her to him with a firm grip on her arms.

On a note of pleading, as he drew her closer, she said, 'Thad . . . ?' Not knowing, really, what she was pleading for, except that she was afraid he wanted, somehow, to hurt her, to punish her for some unwitting crime.

But even if she could have formulated the words, he gave her no chance to use them. One arm encircled her, pulling her against his body, and the other hand was behind her head, holding it firmly while he kissed her unmercifully, ignoring her frightened movement of protest. His mouth tasted, explored, then ruthlessly possessed hers, allowed her no escape, no respite, until she surrendered absolutely and let him take her over completely, bending her body and her will until both were utterly abandoned to him. Blindly she clung to him, and when he was sure she had no wish to escape, no desire to do anything that was not in accord with *his* desires, the hand behind her head moved and began an intimate exploration of her body, lingering over curves and hollows as he moulded her pliant contours even closer into the hard, muscular outlines of his own.

If she moaned it was with pleasure, but the sound that moved her curved throat and mingled with his breath must have prompted him to end the seemingly endless intoxication of the kiss. He held her away from him, his eyes black and unfathomable on her flushed face, the tingling redness of her lips, the languorous, loving, sweet excitement in her eyes.

'Yes,' he said softly. 'Yes. That's what you look like when you've just been thoroughly kissed.'

He only removed his hands, but she swayed as if she had been pushed from him. 'I'm going to do some work,' he said, and walked away, down the passageway to his workroom.

Not quite comprehending what he was doing to her, she

followed him with her eyes. 'Thad——' she said, her voice husky, puzzled as she turned to him. 'It's very late. Aren't you coming to bed?'

With his hand on the door knob he turned and looked at her. The shiver started in the pit of her stomach and began climbing to her shoulders before he spoke, as she anticipated his answer. Finally he said, 'No—thanks,' and went into his room and shut the door.

Her shoulders shuddered, and she clutched at them, her arms crossed and hugging herself, as she stood where he had left her, alone with her terrible humiliation. His brutal cruelty far surpassed anything Ross had done to her. She felt battered and bruised, even beyond resentment or anger. She was too bewildered for that.

Her shawl lay on the hall table where Thad had thrown it down. She looked at it dully for several seconds, then reached out and picked it up, carefuly folding it. She stared down at it for a while, noting the intricate, cobwebby pattern. It was hand spun wool, and she had bought it from a market stall in one of Auckland's handcraft markets. She remembered taking it to the hospital to show Thad, and how he had stroked the fine, soft folds and then lifted his hand to do the same to her hair, as though comparing them. How tender he had been then ...

It was an effort to make her feet carry her into the bedroom, and once there she automatically put away the shawl and undressed, hanging up her dress and placing her shoes neatly side by side in the bottom of the wardrobe. She washed the make-up off her face and got ready for bed. Amazingly, once she lay down between the cool sheets, she was overtaken by a complete and delicious drowsiness. With relief she realised that she was going to be able to sleep, after all.

Her eyes were drooping when a sudden thought shot into her consciousness, for just an instant bringing her eyes wide open in horror, her heart thumping. Surely—*surely* Thad had not been *planning* this devastation since last week? There had been no tangible reason for his sudden new gentleness since then. Had it all been an act?

No. No! Her mind instinctively rejected the fugitive thought. *No.* That couldn't be true. Something had gone wrong tonight, that was all. Perhaps he had not wanted to leave his modelling, his new project. He had, after all, returned to it now, in the early hours of the morning, it was apparently so important to him. And having drunk more than was good for him, and finding Bret kissing her—albeit only a quick peck on the forehead—his latent jealousy of his brother had surfaced, and he had wanted to punish her—take out not only that but his other frustrations on her. It was unfair, but human, and common enough. Tomorrow, he might be regretful ... tomorrow ...

She was wakened by the shrill, insistent ringing of the telephone, and as she sat up, noting the time on the bedside clock that had not yet rung its alarm, she wondered who could be ringing so early. She heard Thad lift the phone and speak into it just as she realised that the other side of bed had not been slept in.

It would not be slept in tonight either. Thad planned to leave this morning for Rotorua and return on Sunday with his exhibits from the show, having taken in the last two days of it.

The phone pinged down, and he came into the bedroom. In the doorway he paused, looking at her. He still wore the shirt and trousers he had worn to the party, but the shirt was half unbuttoned and there were smudges of clay on the sleeves.

'Have you been up all night?' asked Vanessa.

'Most of it.'

He came into the room and got his electric shaver and took it into the bathroom. She heard it whirring, then the sound of the shower, and he came back into the bathroom wearing nothing but a towel tucked around his waist.

'Who was on the telephone?' she asked, as he rummaged in a drawer and pulled out some underpants and socks, and took some shirts and trousers from the wardrobe.

'Celine,' he said. He dropped the towel on the bed and began dressing, pulling on underpants and trousers and shrugging into a cream shirt, bending to pull on socks and shoes.

'Is anything wrong?'

Casting her a slightly impatient glance, he said, 'No. She just wanted to know if I could bring her and her stuff home, that's all.'

'Why? What's the matter with their car?'

He finished buttoning his shirt and turned to take an overnight bag from the top of the wardrobe, tossing it on to the end of the bed.

'She doesn't have it,' he explained curtly. He began putting things into the bag. 'Ritchie unexpectedly had to sail earlier than planned.'

'How on earth did they find him in Rotorua?' she asked.

Thad was opening drawers now, rummaging through them, in search of something. 'He had to leave the address with them,' he said impatiently. 'It's one of the conditions of service.'

'So Ritchie took the car?' she guessed.

'That's right. Any *more* questions?' He was still searching his drawers, obviously getting exasperated.

About to ask him, *What are you looking for?* Vanessa clamped her lips tight and got out of bed, pulling on a silky black robe over her nightgown.

Then, as the possible implications began to hit her, something seemed to burst inside her in an explosion of anger and resentment.

'*Yes.*' she said. 'Are you looking forward to spending the weekend with Celine—*without* her husband?'

He straightened and turned slowly to look at her, brows drawn together, his stance aggressive. He looked dangerous as he said, also slowly, 'And what is that supposed to mean?'

It was too late to back down now. On the flimsiest evidence, he had practically accused her of holding her marriage vows cheap. Well, he wasn't the only one with grounds for suspicion. Anger made her defiant and rash.

'It means just what you think it means!' she told him. 'You said last night that some women don't set much store by a wedding ring. I know Celine is one of them ...'

'*Shut up!*' he snapped, his face white with fury. 'You've got a nerve, you little bitch, accusing Celine—*and* me——!' He took a step forward and she involuntarily flinched from the look on his face. 'Well, whatever you say of me, I won't allow you to fling mud at *her*, do you hear? Her moral standards are considerably better than yours. Some women, though *you* may find it hard to believe, are capable of fidelity, Vanessa, even for quite long periods. So *don't* judge everyone by your own rather pathetic performance as a wife!' He turned and picked up the bag, not bothering to zip it up, and grabbed a jacket from a hanger.

He walked out without even saying goodbye, without so

much as a glance back at her. She heard the car start, then he backed it down the drive and took off with a roar down the road.

Vanessa sank down on the edge of the bed and dropped her head into her hands. Thad's defence of Celine had been as vehement as his condemnation of herself. Was he in love with Celine? Certainly he had left Vanessa in no doubt that he despised *her*! She wasn't, apparently, good enough to tie Celine's shoe. And he believed her unfaithful, incapable of fidelity. *Why?* Surely not because Bret had kissed her forehead, merely. There had to be more to it than that.

Vaguely, she wondered if the accident had had some effect on Thad's mind. Surely such extreme suspicion, on so little evidence, was abnormal?

Tiredly, she rose from the bed and began to dress. It didn't bear thinking about, at all, but she had to go to work today, at least. She would tell Ross she was leaving, but she couldn't do so without notice. Not for his sake, but because it was unfair to leave extra work for the rest of the staff until a replacement could be found.

The bedroom looked mildly chaotic, with the unmade bed that still held the towel Thad had carelessly thrown there; and the drawers that Thad had left half open in his hasty search. She didn't know if he had found what he had been looking for.

A cup of coffee seemed in order before she made the bed and tidied the room. She went to the kitchen and made it, forcing herself to eat some toast at the same time, because the rest of the day would not be easy and it was foolish to add to her troubles by deliberate starvation.

She washed up and made her way back down the passageway, pausing at the door of Thad's workroom. Presumably he had slept on the rather lumpy divan in there. She pushed open the door and saw that he had plumped up the cushion against one end and neatly folded the spare blankets at the other. The lumpy shape of the figure he had been working on, covered by a damp, greyish cloth, sat on the table.

Curiously, she wondered if he had finished, and what it was that had kept him up all night in a fever of creative industry. She crossed to the table and lifted the cloth, then pulled it right back.

At first she just stared at it in non-comprehension, then as the meaning of the thing seeped into her numbed brain, she held her hands to her mouth as a wave of revulsion swept over her.

It was a nude figure, but a caricature, every curve and line exaggerated into something grossly sensual rather than beautiful. The head was back and slightly to one side, and there was in the half-closed eyes and opened lips a strong hint of slyness as well as an almost animal carnality. And in spite of the exaggeration that pervaded the whole thing, the features were undoubtedly hers.

She recalled the way Thad had looked at her last night, just before he came in here, as though he was memorising her face. And his voice saying, '*Yes. That's what you look like when you've just been thoroughly kissed.*'

'*No!* Oh, no!' she whimpered aloud. If *this* was how Thad saw her, what chance on earth did their marriage have? This totally unloving, cruel caricature of the loving face she turned to him when he held her in his arms symbolised his feelings about her, reinforcing the impression of her character that his angry words had given her this morning.

She had a deep sense of being wronged, the unfairness of

it bringing to the surface, eventually, a blazing anger. How did he *dare* to judge her so, with so little reason? How dared he fashion this monstrous, mute clay *lie* to accuse her?

An almost overwhelming urge possessed her to destroy it, to push her hands into the still-damp clay and obliterate the hateful face, the vulgar curves of the body ... With an effort she controlled her shaking fingers and draped the cloth back over the figure instead. Even now she could not quite bring herself to spoil something Thad had spent so many hours working on, even though she hated the result, and shuddered to think that he might ever display it.

She left the room and shut the door behind her with a snap.

In the bedroom she automatically picked up the slightly damp towel from the bed and folded it, then took it into the bathroom to put it away. It was unusual for Thad to be so untidy, but then, this morning had been unusual in many respects.

In the bathroom mirror her face looked pale and her eyes shadowed. She looked at herself searchingly, unable to find any trace of the vulgar cunning she had seen on the clay face in the other room ...

That's what you look like when you've just been thoroughly kissed ...

Compressing her lips, she turned away. It did no good thinking about it. They would have to have things out in some way when Thad came home. In the meantime, there were other, pressing if less important things to do.

She made the bed and then turned her attention to the chest of drawers that held Thad's clothes, that he had not shut properly before he left. The first one was just slightly open, and she closed it and turned to the next. There were clothes spilling out of it, and pulled about untidily in the drawer. She supposed he had been looking for pyjamas. A bundle of letters and cards was in among the clothes, pulled to the fore in his hurry, and the rubber band that secured them was almost pulled off. She picked up the bundle to secure the band, but it had been overstretched, and at her touch it snapped, sending the whole lot cascading to the floor.

Sighing with exasperation, she bent to pick them up. They were the cards and letters Thad had received in the hospital, and she recalled that he had promised to let her have the cards for the hospital appeal. He must have forgotten to sort them out, because the bundle had looked quite untouched.

She picked up an envelope and a flimsy scrap of typing paper fell out of it and floated to the ground, opening out of its single fold. She stretched out her hand to pick it up—and froze, staring at the typed capitals across the paper.

'WHILE YOU LIE THERE YOUR WIFE IS PLAYING AROUND WITH ANOTHER MAN.'

It was unbelievable. She had no experience of anonymous letters, but this—*poison*—unmistakably was one.

With shaking fingers she looked through the rest of the bundle. There were five more envelopes with the typewritten address to the hospital and those beastly little slips of paper, suggesting that she was finding consolation elsewhere while Thad lay tied to a hospital bed. They were not obscene, but the implications were quite clear. SHE'S NOT THE FAITHFUL TYPE: and SHE HAD HIM AT YOUR HOUSE LAST NIGHT: and the one that shocked her most: HE WAS HER LOVER BEFORE. NOW HE IS AGAIN.

'Oh, God! No!' she heard herself whisper. Who could

hate Thad enough to subject him to this when he was ill? Who would be callous enough, sick enough in their mind to do this to anyone? *And how could he have believed them?* Because he had, that was blindingly obvious.

But of course, he *had* been ill, and confined as he was to the unnatural, small world of the hospital, it would have been easy for these filthy things to prey on his mind. She remembered his self-consciousness about his scars, and felt ill when she read the note that said: SHE LIKES MEN WHOLE AND HANDSOME.

If only he had told her, she could have put his fears at rest, she knew she could have. Instead he had let them gnaw away at him, make him suspicious, take away his trust in her. She put them back into the envelopes and placed them carefully on the dressing table. The other letters and cards she bound with another rubber band and replaced in the drawer. There was another envelope in the bottom of the drawer, similar to the ones that contained the anonymous letters, but this one was addressed to the house, with a later postmark.

Vanessa picked it up, remembering a day when Thad had mistakingly put a letter in with hers, and had acted strangely after she had handed it to him, going abruptly out of the room. And afterwards he had been short with her. She remembered the look of the letter, a flimsy single sheet.

Carefully she drew it out, and she was right. It said: SHE'S STILL SEEING HIM. YOU SHOULD KNOW.

The hypocrisy of that sickened her. She stood staring down at the plain white envelopes and wondering who on earth—*who*?

Someone who knew about her past connection with Ross, apparently. That could be anyone who heard the gossip circulating years ago. But ... fragments of an overheard conversation filtered into her brain. Ross, and the promotion he had got over old Mr Carpenter's head. And some suggestion of an anonymous letter to the Head Office having been a factor in the matter.

Ross. Ross, who benefited from the nasty little tales about his rival for a job he wanted. Ross, who admitted that he still wanted her, whom she had been fool enough to believe when he said he had changed, had offered her a job from the kindness of his heart and a desire to make reparation for the petty revenge he had taken on her years before. Ross, who had hinted that he knew her marriage was far from perfect, and in spite of his promise that there would be no strings attached to the job, had used his position and his proximity to try to bring her back to himself.

His arrogance, which she had known so well, would not let him admit that any woman did not ultimately find him irresistible. What an idiot she had been to give credence to his apparent change of character!

Shock and revulsion gave way in time to cold rage. Her first impulse to burn the letters gave way to a cool resolve to take them with her and confront Ross with them.

When she marched into his office as soon as he arrived, taking her handbag with her, and said, 'Would you please ask your secretary not to disturb us for ten minutes?' he looked up and smiled at her. Vanessa realised with revulsion that he thought her request was for quite another reason than the one she actually had in mind. But he did as she asked.

He came round his desk, holding out his hand to her, and she pulled out the seven envelopes from her bag and slapped them on to his palm.

His face stiffened. 'What's this?' he asked.

'I think you know,' Vanessa answered.

He looked down at the top envelope. 'Letters to your husband?' he asked. 'Does he know you're passing on his private correspondence to me?'

'But you wrote them, didn't you? So you already know what's in them.'

'*I* wrote to your husband? My dear, whatever makes you think I did? Is my name on them?'

'They're anonymous letters,' Vanessa said. 'About my supposed involvement with *you*.'

'I'm afraid I don't understand. Why should I write your husband anonymous letters of scandal about myself?'

'To make trouble between Thad and me. You hoped to break up our marriage, didn't you? You said you wanted me for yourself.'

Ross began pulling out and reading the slips of paper from the envelopes.

'I'd always understood anonymous letters were supposed to be a woman's weapon,' he murmured.

'So is gossip,' she said. 'But men as well as women indulge in it.' She told him about the conversation she had overheard in the bank courtyard, and reiterated her reasons for suspecting him.

'My dear girl,' he protested, 'surely you of all people have reason to suspect the truth of malicious gossip.'

That gave her pause, and he followed up his advantage. 'You're jumping to conclusions, Vanessa. There is no evidence to suggest who wrote these. It could have been anyone.'

'It was someone with access to a typewriter,' she said. 'Someone who knew about—my previous relationship with you.' Remembering another point, she added, 'And who knew that you came to my house the night of the staff Christmas party. There was a letter dated the following day.' She picked up the envelope, confirming the postmark she had barely noticed. 'If I took these letters to the police, I expect they would find they were written on a typewriter from the bank.'

'The police?' Ross repeated sharply. 'Don't be ridiculous! None of these could be called threatening letters, and sending anonymous information is hardly illegal. Besides, the entire bank staff has access to the typewriters. I doubt very much if anyone would believe *I* had written these—as against, say, a junior member of the female staff. Someone who may well be jealous of your looks or perhaps has what might be called a crush on me. And these letters don't, actually, identify the man.'

Remembering the adoring looks cast in his direction by some of the younger girls, Vanessa had to admit to herself that the case against one of them would be more convincing than against a bank manager accused of writing anonymous accusations against himself. Except that she knew the girls and didn't believe them capable of such malice.

'I've always heard that the proper place for these things is the rubbish bin,' said Ross, gathering them up. 'Shall I oblige?'

'No.' She took them from him.

He shrugged. 'Very well. But if you take my advice, you'll tear them up and endeavour to forget them.'

'This kind of thing isn't easy to forget,' she said bitterly.

'Thad finds it difficult, does he?' Ross asked, his tone sympathetic.

He was turning away from her, but fleetingly she caught the very slight hint of a smile on his face, and in that moment she knew that although he denied, it, she was right in her conviction that he had written the letters. She had seen that expression before, when he was particularly pleased with himself over some clever ploy.

She would never be able to prove it, and she could think of no way in which she might compel him to admit to Thad that they were based on lies. It was probably true that simply writing anonymous letters was not illegal, but even if it was against the law, the single constable in Aputa was probably not qualified to handle such things, and bringing in experts would set tongues wagging and cause a lot of bother, with probably the very result that Ross had prophesied. He was admitting nothing, and never would, and he was clever enough to have covered his tracks. If the blame was ever laid, it would be on some innocent person.

Seething inwardly, she put the letters back in her bag and said, 'I was going to give my notice this morning, anyway. This is as good a time as any.'

Ross turned to face her. 'You're leaving?' He looked annoyed. 'You'll have to work out a week's notice.'

'Yes, I know that.' She turned to go. 'Thank you for giving me the job, Ross, but I don't need it now.'

'Like me,' he said.

'What?' Vanessa paused at the door.

'You're throwing over the job, just as you threw me over once,' he said. 'You were pleased enough to get it when I offered it to you. I don't suppose it matters to you that you're going to be difficult to replace within a week.'

'I'm afraid not,' she said. 'Not for your sake, Ross. Quite frankly, I don't think I owe you a thing.'

She mentioned the fact of her leaving casually to one of the other women on the staff, and the news was soon common knowledge. Vanessa was surprised and pleased to have several people indicate their regret at the news.

'Your husband's getting enough out of his pottery to make you a lady of leisure, is he?' one of the men teased.

Vanessa smiled. 'I doubt if I shall have much leisure,' she said. She was, in fact, hoping that another job might present itself soon, but she didn't want to mention that. 'But Thad is doing quite well, yes.'

'Didn't I hear that he went to that exhibition in Rotorua?' someone asked. 'I read something about it the other day in the paper, and I'm sure someone said they'd heard your husband was there—and that red-headed girl ...'

'That's right,' Vanessa said evenly, hiding the emotion that started. 'We all went down last weekend, and Thad has returned to the exhibition today, to pick up his things.'

'Oh, I thought it was on until tomorrow—the show.'

'Yes. He comes home on Sunday,' Vanessa told her.

One of the other girls, newly married, asked, 'Aren't you nervous, left on your own? I'd hate Roger to go away and leave me for a weekend.'

Vanessa laughed. 'Not really. There's very little crime in Aputa. And I got used to being on my own when Thad was in hospital.'

'Yes, I suppose so ...' The girl turned and smiled at Ross who had emerged from his office holding a sheaf of papers which he placed on her desk.

He gave her his most charming smile and asked, 'Think you can deal with them before closing time, Marilyn?'

'Sure, Mr Bray.' Marilyn gave him a dazzling smile back. She was madly in love with her Roger, Vanessa knew, but even she was not totally impervious to Ross. No wonder the man was so galled at her own total indifference.

CHAPTER NINE

AMONG the mail that Vanessa took from the letterbox when she got home was one of the distinctive envelopes from the state insurance people, addressed to Thad. It didn't need to be opened for her to guess with some accuracy that it contained a cheque. Their financial difficulties would probably be solved by that, since it was almost certainly the long-awaited compensation for Thad's injuries.

But the whole future of their marriage, she felt, was still in jeopardy. She was pinning her hopes on being able to persuade Thad that there was no truth in the horrible things those letters had suggested, counting on his being able to *see* the truth, once the whole sordid business was brought into the open.

Sometimes his lack of faith brought a wave of anger washing over her, but she damped it down, determined not to make matters worse by a display of temper. Surely calm discussion would be more productive than recriminations, she told herself firmly. A blazing row might relieve her feelings, but it would not do much for their relationship.

The evening seemed to drag, and about ten she decided to prepare for bed, taking a long warm bath in scented water to pass the time and calm her jumping nerves. She put on a nightgown, one of the filmy wisps of chiffon and lace she had bought for her honeymoon, and covered it with her black silk wrap. A warm drink might help her sleep, she decided, and going into the kitchen she put on the electric jug and prepared a cup of instant coffee.

As she was replacing the jug on the bench, a car purred down the driveway, and incredibly she heard it drive straight into the garage that Thad had left open that morning.

He had come home—tonight! Surprise, then rising hope, kept her still and listening. She heard a car door close with a snap, and knew that in moments he would be coming inside. Had he regretted the things he had said to her this morning? Was he, too, anxious to clear the air, to repair the ravages that had lately taken place in their relationship? He could only have spent a few hours, at most, in Rotorua before turning round and returning home.

She took down another cup and spooned coffee hastily into it, stirring water and sugar in the way Thad like it. Carefully she put both cups on the table as soft footfalls sounded outside. Anticipatory visions danced into her mind of the two of them sitting with steaming mugs in their hands, talking quietly of what had gone wrong between them—putting it right.

She flew to the door to open it and save him using his key, and seeing the dark, tall shadow just reaching the step, threw the door wide, and stepped back, then moved forward, ready to greet him with an embrace—and stopped short as the man crossed the threshold and pushed the door to behind him.

'Ross!'

'I must admit I hadn't expected quite such an eager greeting,' drawled Ross. 'Thanks for letting me in, Vanessa.'

'What do you want?' she asked sharply. 'I thought you were Thad.'

'But you're not expecting him until Sunday.'

'No, I wasn't, but when I heard the car—you parked in the garage!' she said accusingly.

'Yes, I did. It was conveniently empty, and my car can't be seen from the road, there.' His eyes wandered over her with a suggestiveness she hated.

'You're not *staying*!'

'Don't worry, I'll go before morning,' he smiled confidently.

'You'll go *now*! I don't want you here—what on earth do you think you're doing, barging in here at this time of the night?'

'My dear, it was an opportunity too good to be missed. I told you, I want you, Vanessa. And you want me, too, don't you?'

'No!'

He reached a hand towards her and she backed away from him.

'Don't be coy,' he said, and followed her, until she found herself against the table.

With gritted teeth she said, 'I am not being coy! It was all over between us years ago, Ross. *Please* understand that. Please go away and leave me alone.'

'You don't mean that.' His hand reached out again, and as she swiftly evaded it he lunged for her, coming up against the table. She caught a whiff of whisky on his breath, and realised he had been drinking.

'Ross, I swear I'll scream if you touch me. I mean it.'

'So what?' he sneered, a glitter of derision in his blue eyes. 'The neighbours are going to come running, you accuse me of rape—and who's going to believe you? My reputation in this town is impeccable, Vanessa. I've seen to that—my career matters to me——'

'Then how can you risk a rape charge?'

'How can you risk bringing one? Wasn't it you who asked for a very private, uninterrupted interview with me this morning—so that you could let me know your husband was going away? And who just let me in?'

'That's not true! You must have heard me telling the others——'

'Your word against mine, Vanessa. The word of a girl whose reputation is hardly spotless——'

'Thanks to *you*! And all that was *years* ago.'

'Mud sticks—for a long time.'

'It might stick to you, too—even if you were not found guilty.'

'Well, the question won't arise, because I'm not going to rape you, Vanessa. You're going to co-operate—willingly.'

'You're mad!' she exclaimed. 'Even if I wasn't married to Thad, I'd never let you touch me again—I find your conceit laughable, and your kisses repulsive!'

His eyes flared with anger, then he lunged at her and grabbed her arm, and her hair, twisting her wrist up behind her back, and stifling her involuntary cry by jerking her against him so hard and suddenly that the breath was momentarily knocked out of her.

'Scream and I'll break your arm!' he gritted, and looking at the near-snarl on his face, she believed him. It might come to that yet, but she hoped not. Surely there was some way to reason him out of this.

'If you do,' she said, 'you can hardly expect me to be very—co-operative, can you?'

The whisky on his breath nauseated her. She turned her face away, and he pulled her hair with a jerk so that she had to face him again.

It had been stupid to make him angry, she supposed. He had obviously been drinking, and although the neighbours might hear if she screamed, it was not at all certain—the houses were not very close.

She didn't know how much whisky he had drunk, but it was evidently enough to make him careless of the consequences to himself if his plans misfired—or over-confident in her eventual capitulation to either persuasion or force.

'Don't turn your face away from me!' he snapped angrily.

'It's the whisky——' she gasped. 'You've been drinking, and I don't like the smell. Please, can't we sit down and have some coffee?' She had to keep her wits about her and try guile, because there was no way she could fight his strength. With an effort she produced a small, rather trembly smile. 'You're hurting me, Ross—you don't really want to hurt me, do you?' The coaxing, pleading note she forced into her voice nauseated her, but the tears she allowed to gather in her eyes were genuine enough. He *was* hurting her, and she was frightened.

She could see that he didn't quite trust her about-face, but his hold loosened a little, and she took advantage of it to slip out of his arms, careful not to move violently, and sat down at the table, motioning him to take the other chair.

Ross moved it so that it was closer to her, and between her and the outer door, then he pulled the other cup towards himself, and as she lifted hers and managed to force down a sip or two he followed suit, watching her warily over the rim of the cup.

The success of her ploy surprised her, and gave her a little confidence. Less terrified now, she lowered her eyes and tried to think logically what her next step should be. She gulped down some more of the coffee and shot a glance at him, trying to gauge his mood.

He was looking back to her with a smile, and the cruel

amusement in his eyes seemed to indicate that he knew quite well what he was doing—simply playing a cat and mouse game with her, until it suited him to pounce ...

Panic took hold of her again, and when he drained his cup and placed it with an air of finality on the table she jumped up, saying hastily, 'I'll get you another.'

But his hand shot out and grasped her wrist, jerking her off balance on to his knees. His arm clamped about her, pinning her free one, while his hand still pinioned her wrist. She turned away from his face as it neared hers, trying to struggle out of his grip, but aware that it was useless.

Then he seemed suddenly to still, his head jerking up, and Vanessa stopped struggling, realising he had heard something, turning her own head in surprised hope towards the door, as it opened and Thad stood framed against the darkness outside.

Her first emotion was overwhelming relief, and joy at seeing him. Then her heart thudded with trepidation as she saw the set, white fury on his face and realised what he must be thinking.

Ross said accusingly, turning to her, 'You said he'd be away until *Sunday*!'

His hands fell away as he stood up, and she flew towards Thad, saying in a shaken voice, 'Oh, Thad! I'm so glad to see you!'

She had her hand reaching out to him, almost touching his shirt, before the contempt in his eyes, and the sound of his harsh voice stopped her in her tracks.

'You don't expect me to *believe* that, do you?'

Shocked, she swallowed, and then determinedly moved towards him again. 'Thad—listen——'

He took her shoulders and moved her aside so roughly

that she staggered against the wall. Now she could see Ross, and as he looked at her the amused, rueful smile on his face that suddenly displaced his chagrined anger gave her a hint of what was to follow.

'I'm afraid the cat's out of the bag, darling,' he said. 'In the circumstances you could hardly expect Thad to fall for your welcoming wife act.'

Trying to ignore him, she said pleadingly, 'Thad——'

But he wasn't looking at her. He was looking at Ross, with a hard, still concentration.

Ross interrupted her. 'Sorry, old man,' he said patronisingly to Thad. 'I did try to break it off when you came out of hospital, but Vanessa wouldn't have that—and I admit I find it difficult to resist such a beautiful woman as your wife.'

'Stop it!' Vanessa cried. 'Thad, he's lying! There was nothing to break off.' He did turn to her then, his dark eyes narrow and assessing, and she went on, 'He tried to rape me tonight—oh, Thad, you must believe me!'

'Rape!' Ross sounded outraged. 'Now, wait a minute Vanessa, that's a very serious charge. I'll have to ask you to take that back.'

'No, it's true. You threatened me and twisted my arm——'

Thad's eyes glittered as they swung to Ross, silently demanding his reply.

'Of course it isn't true,' he said calmly. 'Look——' he indicated the two coffee cups on the table. 'She made coffee for me. Is that likely, if I was trying to attack her? She was perfectly willing—in fact this whole thing tonight was her idea.' He turned to Vanessa. 'I'm sorry, my dear,' he said, 'but if you're talking rape, I must defend myself. I wish you'd simply admitted to Thad that we've been having an affair. I'm willing to shoulder part of the blame for that, but I can't allow you to accuse me of a criminal offence.'

Desperately, Vanessa turned to Thad. 'I made coffee for you,' she said. 'When I heard his car I thought you'd come home. We haven't been having an affair—it's all lies.'

Thad suddenly moved, snapping open the door behind him and throwing it wide. His voice dangerously level, he said, 'Get out of here, Bray, before I throw you out.'

Ross took a few hesitant steps forward and stopped just short of the doorway. He looked from Thad to Vanessa and then said, 'I'd like a retraction, Vanessa.'

Stunned by his audacity, she blinked and then said with great clarity, 'Go to hell!'

'I second that,' Thad said quietly.

'You believe her?' Ross said contemptuously. 'You fool! Ask her how I know exactly what your bedroom looks like—there's a picture of a horse on a beach over the bed, the bedspread is purple candlewick, there's a set of sheets that matches it, only a bit paler—she even has a nightdress that goes with them, too—very sexy—it laces down the front——'

Thad made a violent movement, and Ross turned quickly and went through the doorway.

Thad didn't shut the door until the car had backed out of the garage and gone down the drive. Vanessa stayed looking at the taut muscles of his back as he stood looking out into the darkness, his hands resting on his hips.

When the sound of the engine died away, he slammed the door shut and spun round to look at her.

'I won't ask you how he knows,' he said flatly.

Without much hope, because his eyes held a contemptuous anger when they rested on her, Vanessa said, 'Because you believe in me?'

His mouth twisted bitterly. 'No, Because I couldn't stand listening to any more lies.'

She felt bitter herself. Today had been a succession of unpleasant shocks, one after the other. 'If you had any trust in me,' she said, 'you would know I've never lied to you.'

'Trust! That's good, from you. Wasn't it only this morning that you accused me of planning to make love to Celine?'

'I'm not the only one who's been making accusations, Thad. In fact, I could say you started it.'

'And I could say I have better grounds than you did.'

'*What* grounds?' she flashed angrily. 'Anonymous letters?'

The flare of surprise in his eyes quickly died, to be replaced by a knowing cynicism. 'So——' he drawled, 'you took the opportunity of my absence to go through my things'.

'I did not! I found them accidentally when I was tidying up the drawer that you left all up-ended this morning. At least, the first one I found by accident. After that—yes, I looked for the others. They concerned me, after all.' Her voice softened with hurt pleading, as she added, 'Oh, Thad! How could you have taken such—filth seriously?'

He swung away from her, his hands gripping the bench in front of the window, his eyes staring out into the blackness. 'I didn't, at first,' he said, sounding as though the words were dragged out against his will, as though he didn't want to explain but was somehow being compelled to. 'You have no conception of what it was like,' he said. 'Incarcerated in that place day after dreary day, watching you grow more beautiful, more desirable all the time, and not being able to touch you—make love to you as I wanted. You haven't found all the letters. The first two or three I threw away, tore up and got rid of them. I told myself they were nothing to do with us as people—they were the product of some sick mind that fed itself on that kind of trash. Then I began keeping the things, with some vague idea of evidence ... But by then I'd started to analyse what you said to me when you came visiting, watching your expression, wondering if you were really sincere, if you could still feel the same about me, with my scars——'

'Oh, Thad! I told you, they can make no difference——'

He swung round then to face her, his face hard and his eyes darkly glittering. 'You told me so many times I began to wonder if the lady didn't protest too much. Who were you trying to convince, Vanessa? Yourself or me? You were so damned *grateful* to me for saving your life. Well, gratitude doesn't interest me. It wasn't what I wanted.'

'I couldn't help being grateful,' she said. 'But that wasn't the only thing I felt for you.'

'No—I can still make you feel desire for me, can't I? If it's dark, or you can close your eyes.'

Appalled, she stared at him. 'That's nonsense! The day you came home, it was broad daylight, when I——'

'When you closed your eyes tight when I took you in my arms, and had to nerve yourself to open them and look at my face. Oh, it was a good try, you almost had me convinced that you couldn't wait to get me into bed. You were far more forthcoming than you'd ever been before. But then I daresay you may have had some—tuition—from Ross while I was in hospital.'

She shook her head, tired of repeating the denials that he didn't believe, anyway.

'I couldn't bear to take you when all you offered me was gratitude,' he went on. 'I'm sorry I could never bring myself to appreciate your sacrifice, even when you steeled yourself to touch my scars. I should have admired your courage, but all I could do was hate you because you didn't love me.'

'But I did love you,' she protested. 'I still do.'

'So you prove it by inviting your lover into my house and my bed whenever my back is turned?'

'Don't *say* that! Ross is not my lover!'

'No?' Thad looked pointedly at the two coffee cups on the table. 'You made him coffee and sat on his knee because he was raping you? And gave him a guided tour of the bedroom, too?'

'I *said* I made the coffee for *you*! I didn't *expect* anyone else to drive into the garage at this time of night. I opened the door and before I realised who it was, he was in here. He—he tried to persuade me, first. Then he threatened me and tried force. He said if I screamed he'd break my arm. He meant it.'

'And in the middle of all this, the two of you sat down for a friendly cup of coffee and an affectionate cuddle,' he said derisively.

'Oh, you won't try to understand, will you?' she cried with sudden fury. 'You're a man, too—and strong. Well, I'm not! I couldn't fight him—I tried, and he hurt me! So I had to use my wits instead. I hoped the coffee might sober him up—I hoped I could talk him out of it! It might have been stupid and useless, but it was the only thing I could think of.' Possessed now by a fine, fierce rage, she went on recklessly, 'I might have managed it by flattering his vanity. Like you, he has more than his fair share of that.'

'*Like me?*' Thad's step forward was menacing, but she was angry enough to hold her ground, staring back at him defiantly.

'*Yes.* Like you—with your stupid assumption that I

could stop loving you because your body is no longer perfect, and your face is marred. Did you really think I fell in love with your good looks? Thank you for your opinion of my depth of character! I suppose, thinking *that* of me, it was logical to conclude that I was incapable of fidelity, too. And I was fool enough, once, to think that you really loved me!'

Her voice wavered, and she turned away from him, impatiently brushing tears from her eyes, taking a deep breath to stop them coming.

Thad's hands on her shoulders spun her to face him, and she looked defiantly up into the dark, forbidding mask that was his face.

'I loved you,' he said. 'So much that I couldn't leave you even when I was certain you were involved with another man. At first it was only a suspicion that I tried to tell myself wasn't true. And last weekend at Rotorua you were so loving, so open, I persuaded myself I was wrong, that you'd only been a little repelled by what had happened to me, and the rest was imagination. On Mokoia you didn't close your eyes against the sight of me.'

Taking no notice of her whispered protest—'I *never* have!' he went on: 'Then I saw you kissing Bray when he brought you home on Thursday.' His voice hardened, and his hands on her shoulders hurt. 'That was careless, Vanessa. You must have thought me very stupid, or very complaisant, to risk it in front of our own home.'

'How could you have seen?' she said. 'You were in your workroom.'

'Oh, no!' His lips twisted. 'You were late, and I was such an eager husband, this last week, I was actually watching for you from the front window. After seeing you and your lover,' his fingers cruelly stilled her protesting movement, 'exchanging that passionate embrace, I retreated to my workroom.' His eyes changed, becoming a little unfocused. 'Like a wounded animal, I suppose,' he murmured, half to himself. 'Retreating to its lair.'

'You hardly looked at me when I came in,' she said, remembering.

'I saw enough,' he told her harshly. 'That lovely mouth of yours tells on you, when you've been kissed.' He raised his hand and his thumb brushed her lips in a hard caress. 'I badly wanted to do something violent to you.'

Instead, he had made that obscene model. Vanessa flinched away from his touch, and his words, but he caught her hair in his hand and forced her to face him. His eyes seemed to flame with temper.

A little desperately, she said, 'Thad. You were wrong about that kiss. Ross forced it on me unexpectedly. I didn't want it—and I didn't reciprocate.' It crossed her mind that Ross had known Thad was watching, had used the opportunity to drive another wedge of suspicion between them. 'He's been trying to make trouble between us, Thad. You don't know him——'

'And you do. As though I didn't know it.' His hand moved from her hair to the nape of her neck and began moving against her skin rather roughly in an almost involuntary caress that threatened to turn into something else, the thumb finding the cord of her throat and moving up and down on it, as though at any minute it might tighten and try to choke her.

'I used to know him well—or thought I did. Before we were married.'

His smile was mirthless. 'Do you think you need to tell me that?' he demanded cynically. 'Let me assure you, there were any number of people anxious to acquaint me with that interesting fact, among others, before I ever put a ring on your pretty finger.'

So he had been aware all along that Ross was the man in her past. 'I suppose I should have realised,' she said bitterly. 'Someone was bound to make it their business to pass the gossip on to you. I wish you'd let me give you *my* version.' How many men did he think there were?

'I didn't see any point in raking over old coals. Whatever had happened in the past, I believed that once you promised your future to me, I could trust you.'

'What happened to that trust, Thad?' she challenged him softly.

Abruptly he released her, his face hard, eyes glittering coldly.

'It came up against some hard facts,' he said. 'And eventually—shattered.'

'It must have been very fragile. Like your love.'

His jaw tightened. 'Be careful what you say, Vanessa. It wouldn't take much to make me——'

'What?' she taunted. 'Hit me? It couldn't hurt much more than what you've been doing to me over the past few months, with your idiotic suspicion, and your—your so-called lovemaking. Because whatever it was that you were making, it certainly wasn't love!'

'I *said*, be careful,' he said warningly, as their eyes clashed.

'I am *tired* of being careful!' she almost shouted at him. 'I've been careful of your moods, your feelings, your unutterably despicable suspicions, your childishly tender male pride! And what was the result? You come all the way back from Rotorua—or perhaps you never went there, perhaps you've been skulking about all day like some cheap private detective, hoping to catch me out in a "compromising" situation. Well, now you've convinced yourself you've succeeded. *Congratulations!*'

She saw him clench his fist and flinched, although he was not raising it. But when she turned instinctively away, his hard hand on her wrist brought her round roughly to face him again.

His face looked taut and a little pale as he said tightly, 'I was not trying to catch you out. You may laugh, but when I got to Rotorua I began to convince myself that there must be some reasonable explanation for what I'd seen on Thursday, and that I owed it to you to ask for it. I even gave myself a lecture about love and trust, Vanessa, quite equal to yours. But there is a limit. There's a difference between being trusting and being taken for a fool.'

Straining in a futile way against his grip, she said, 'I won't laugh, Thad. I don't find any of this the least bit funny—least of all your complete lack of faith in me.

Even now, as their eyes blazed antagonism and distrust at each other, the nearness of him acted like a drug on her senses. She was torn between the anger that made her want to spit and scratch like a cornered cat, and the quite different desire aroused by the touch of his fingers against her skin, the rise and fall of his broad chest beneath the cotton shirt, the curve of his mouth, even while it twisted with his contempt for her.

His eyes held hers, and her breath quickened, her eyes dilating as she read the answering gleam of awareness in his. Her lips parted on a soft sound of protest, of denial—and he dropped her wrist, almost throwing it from him as he stepped back.

His mouth compressed, and he turned and began to stride towards the outer door. He had already opened it when she managed to ask, 'Where are you going?'

'I'm going to a pub for the night,' he replied in a thickened voice.

'That seems very melodramatic,' she commented. 'Is it necessary?'

Thad's left hand went up to the framework of the door, and he seemed to be leaning on it. Without looking at her, he said, 'Vanessa, I've never struck a woman in my life, and I don't intend to start now. It's one temptation I've been fighting ever since I walked in here. But there is another, which in the circumstances you may regard as perverted. I have a strong desire to take you to bed, and I don't think you would like what would happen to you if I did. I can't guarantee to withstand *that* temptation if I stay here any longer.'

He stood there a moment longer, then straightened and looked back at her, standing still and shocked in her silk gown, with wide, dazed eyes, and her fair hair falling about her shoulders. Then he turned away, but as his foot touched the step she called, 'Thad?'

He stopped without turning, and waited.

Vanessa's courage almost failed her, knowing what she was inviting, but she had an extraordinarily strong conviction that to spend this night apart would widen the rift between them still further, make Thad harden his heart even more against her. Beneath the hurt and anger she knew she loved him and always would, and would dare anything to keep him by her side. His love for her might be mainly physical, but she knew it had the power to hold him even against his better judgment. If it was the only effective weapon she had, she would use it, no matter what it cost her.

Clearly, she said, 'I want you to stay.'

He stiffened, then turned. 'You don't mean that.' His voice was flat, his face expressionless.

Vanessa swallowed and repeated, 'I want you to stay.'

It took some effort to meet his eyes, that suddenly blazed into a dangerous flame.

'Are you prepared to take the consequences?' he asked.

Her throat felt tight, but she managed a husky, 'Yes.'

Thad moved into the room again and shut the door with a soft, final-sounding click behind him. His eyes assessed her with a strange detachment and then he began slowly moving towards her.

She stood her ground, waiting for him, her heart beating in a way that made her conscious of its presence.

He didn't touch her, merely looking, at her face, the proudly tilted chin, the slender, taut neck, the curves of her breasts that moved slightly under the silk, with her quickened breathing. In spite of herself, her agitation must have shown. In a soft, taunting tone he asked, 'Are you sure?'

'I'm sure.'

He smiled, but it did nothing to reassure her. His hands hooked into his belt and he stood with his feet slightly apart in an arrogantly male stance, and Vanessa recalled baiting him with accusations of childishness and stupidity, and other things. His gaze held an insulting intimacy, and she caught her breath, thinking, *My God—what have I done?*

The command came softly, but it was unmistakably a command, and the look on his face reinforced it.

'Wait for me in the bedroom,' he said.

CHAPTER TEN

VANESSA woke with a sense of having slept late. The blinds were still down, but the crack of light that showed at the side of one of them was brilliant with day.

She closed her eyes again as her body came to life. It ached slightly, and she felt bruised and spent. The bird noises outside the window, harsh quarrelling from a couple of starlings, the gossipy twittering of the sparrows and the distinctive fluting tones of the tui that frequented the native trees in the garden, reminded her that was no way to feel in the morning.

She knew without looking that Thad had left her side some time ago. She threw her arm over her closed eyes, trying to shut out the daylight, cowering from facing what the day might bring. Last night she had taken a desperate gamble. She didn't yet know if she had won the toss.

Behind closed eyelids, memory replayed the climactic events of the night.

Thad's quiet order to wait for him had stirred a flash of rebellion, and for a moment she had considered defying him, but, aware that whatever happened she had brought it on herself, and determined to follow through with whatever her desperate courage had brought, she had turned and walked down the passage, her head high, not looking back. She knew he was watching from the kitchen doorway, until she went into the bedroom.

She had switched on the bedside light and heard him go into his workroom, making her straighten and stand listening, wondering what he intended to do in there. She remembered the thing under the cloth that stood on the table there, and shuddered, picturing him standing there looking at that, then coming to her ...

Deliberately she stiffened her back and crossed to the window to open it, for the room seemed stifling and muggy. She drew up the blind a little to enable her to reach the catch, and stood in the faint breeze, letting it cool her face and throat.

Minutes passed, and she found the tension so intense she clenched her hands tightly together to stop herself from breaking into some form of hysteria. How long did he mean to keep her waiting? Was this part of Thad's punishment of her, a deliberate assault on her nerves? Perhaps he intended her to wait all night, or until she could stand the suspense no longer. Was he waiting for her to come running down the passageway to him, begging him to get it over with?

When at last she heard the click of the door, an involuntary shiver ran over her entire body. She stood unmoving by the window, sure that the small current of cool air was the only thing that kept her from fainting.

His footsteps were not hurried, but she heard every one clearly, and when he shut the bedroom door decisively it seemed to release something in her, and she swung round to look at him.

He was pulling open the buttons on his shirt, leaving faint dark smudges on it, because he had been doing something with the clay, and there was still some on his hands. He threw off the shirt impatiently, in the direction of the bed, but when it fell on the floor he didn't bother to pick it up. He hadn't taken his eyes off her since he entered the room. His expression was grim, but there was an angry desire in his eyes.

He came over to her and, standing close, reached out and pulled down the blind. Without haste he hooked his fingers into the tie belt of her robe and pulled it undone. The edges parted, revealing a glimpse of the flimsy gown beneath.

'Take it off,' Thad said, and watched critically as she slid the robe off her shoulders and let it fall softly to the carpet.

With his hands on either side of her face he brought her close to him, sliding his thumbs over her cheeks and into the hollows beneath her ears. She remembered the clay on his fingers as she felt the slight, slippery dampness against her skin, and wondered if he had deliberately not thoroughly washed it off. Did he want to smear her with—mud?

She closed her eyes against the horrible thought, and his hands moved to her shoulders. Harshly he ordered, '*Don't close your eyes*. Not yet.'

Helplessly, she opened them again and looked at him. His fingers moved the thin straps on her shoulders, pulling them down over her arms so that the bodice slipped down and exposed the top of her breasts. Instinctively she put up a hand to stop it moving further down, and Thad smiled in a mocking way, moving his hands again, one spreading against the bareness of her back and the other sliding under her chin as he raised her face to his. '*Now*,' he said, as his lips closed on hers, and she closed her eyes.

His mouth was hard and utterly ruthless, without tenderness of any sort, without mercy. She felt breathless and battered, and when his hand slid down her throat and impatiently pushed her hand from the bodice that she held over her breasts, her resistance was feeble and futile. The fabric, too, was pushed away, and his hand, with merciless expertise, brought her soft flesh to a singing excitement.

In spite of that, the quality of his lovemaking shocked and angered her. It was devastatingly sensual, but with an element of subjugation that she could not accept.

His hand moved down her back, and was stopped by the edge of the nightgown. Reluctantly he released her mouth and with his hands on her waist, muttered, 'Take the damned thing off.'

But she was pulling it up again to cover her, and as she fumbled for the straps, he caught her hand and said, 'I told you to take it off!'

'So that you can stand there watching me, like a connoisseur in a strip club?' she asked angrily.

He jerked her hand away, pulling down the filmy ruffles again so roughly that she heard some stitching give way.

Unthinking, she raised her free hand and slapped him hard. He tossed back his head a little as though the sting of it was no more than an annoying insect bite. 'You said you'd take whatever comes,' he drawled.

'I didn't say I'd be your willing slave!' she spat at him.

'But that's the thing about slaves,' he said. 'Isn't it? It makes no difference if they're willing or not.'

In spite of her furious struggles, he picked her up in his hard, powerful arms and carried her over to the bed.

Vanessa lowered her arm from her eyes and examined it curiously, surprised to find no mark on the faintly tanned skin. There was faint bruising on one shoulder, but that had happened in the kitchen, before that devastating lovemaking took place. She sat up, running her hands gingerly over her naked body, seeing the crumpled little heap of lace and chiffon that was the disputed nightgown, lying on the floor. Of course, Thad had got his way in the end.

There was a faintly blue patch on the curve of her left

breast, but otherwise she seemed to have escaped remarkably lightly, considering ...

She shivered with the memory, and threw back the blankets, looking round for her robe. It still lay by the window, and she padded over the carpet and picked it up to don it over her nakedness. She had a shower and brushed her hair, listening in spite of herself for sounds of Thad moving about. Surely he hadn't left?

Not waiting to dress, she went swiftly down the passageway, and pushed open the door of his workroom.

She supposed she should have knocked. He was dressed, but not working. He sat at the table, his head buried in his hands, shoulders hunched, in an attitude that shouted mutely of some terrible despair.

He must have sensed her shocked presence, for after a few moments he raised his head and looked at her. He stood up slowly, fumbling a little with the chair. Vanessa didn't remember ever seeing him make a clumsy movement before.

'Vanessa!' he said. 'Are you all right?' He looked at her wan face and the faint shadows about her eyes, and said with a twisted smile, 'No, of course you're not. I hurt you. I *meant* to hurt you.'

She moved hesitantly into the room, and he said explosively, '*God*! how you must hate me!'

'Is that what you wanted?' she asked.

For a moment he was silent; then he said, slowly and clearly, 'I wanted—to hurt you. I deliberately took you as brutally as I could, even though I knew that you must loathe me for it. Perhaps that *is* what I wanted, deep down. Because I couldn't stand your pity.'

Did he still think she had only pitied him, only been grateful?

There was pain in his dark eyes, and she looked away

from it. The mound of clay under the damp cloth caught her eyes, but there was something different about the outline.

She walked over to the table and lifted the cloth. The mound of clay was just that, a shapeless lump of greyish, damp, smooth clay. A quick glance around showed her no sign of the nude figure in the room.

'You destroyed it,' she said.

'You saw it?' His voice sounded strained. 'I'm sorry. You weren't meant to.'

'It will teach me not to pry, won't it?' she shrugged, trying to achieve a light note. 'It was—quite a revelation—on how you see me.'

He was standing half behind her, and as she dropped the cloth and turned, he put his hand on her arm and quickly took it away again.

'I hoped that destroying that might be enough, last night,' he said. 'I tried to wreak my feelings on it instead of you. It didn't entirely work.'

'No. You did a fair amount of—of wreaking on me, too, didn't you?'

'I know an apology would be ludicrously inadequate,' he said. 'No man has the right to do what I did to a woman—no matter what she's done.'

'I thought—you'd persuaded yourself that I deserved it,' she said. 'You did warn me, after all.'

'That's what I told myself last night,' he said. He wasn't looking at her. His eyes were fixed on the clay-smeared table as he asked, 'Why did you ask me to stay, Vanessa?'

'Because,' she said softly, 'I love you.'

He turned his eyes to her then, with a searching, intent look. 'Even after last night?' he queried softly.

'After—this morning,' she corrected gently.

Last night she had hated him for a time, for his cruelty and his disbelief, but in the early hours, when he turned in the dim light and found her lying awake with the tears falling softly on the pillow, he had very slowly raised his hand and gently brushed them away with his fingers. She had lain perfectly still, afraid to believe in that gentleness, and he moved closer and softly gathered her into his arms and began stroking her hair. His lips brushed her still-damp cheek, and when she made no demur, settled lightly on her mouth. No response was forthcoming, and after a few moments he lifted his mouth from hers and she felt his chest rise and fall in a sigh. He still held her, his arms keeping her close to the warmth of his body. She felt his breath on her temple, but he made no attempt to kiss her again.

Gradually the stiffness of her body melted against him, and it came to her that he was silently asking for forgiveness. Fear and bitterness ebbed away, and she made a slight, deliberate movement that brought her soft form curving closer into his, then she moved her hands from their resting place against his chest, to his shoulders and then his neck.

Thad drew in a sharp breath and lifted his head to look at her face. She looked back at him gravely, until he gradually lowered his mouth to hers, touching it tentatively, as though assuring her she could draw back. Every move he made was like that, the complete opposite of last night's fiercely self-willed possession of her. There was to be nothing, this time, but what she wanted, not one further intimacy without her tacit permission. Even as the flame of his passion burned high and hard, she sensed the element of iron control, that he had before deliberately unleashed. This time she knew that right up until the very last second she could have stopped him with a word—a gesture, even—the slightest hint of denial. But she didn't.

That was what gave her hope now. For surely there had been more than a gesture of reparation, in that tenderness and determination to restore the self-respect that he had deliberately and brutally torn from her. Surely, this time, there had been an element of something more than a merely sexual love.

'You're very generous,' Thad said tersely, now. 'More so than I have been.'

'Thank you,' she said, with a touch of wryness. She could have done without the compliment, if he had said he loved her. But he had said that last night, citing as proof the fact that he had stayed with her while he believed her to have another lover, that he had been willing to listen to her explanation of Ross's kiss—until he had come home and found her with Ross in a far more damning situation.

She said, 'There's something I have to tell you——'

His face hardened and he turned away. Swiftly she added, 'I think I have the right to ask you to listen. Please look at me.'

Thad seemed to brace himself before he turned in obedience to her calm request. 'When I took the job at the bank, I didn't know that you'd heard anything about Ross and me. He spread a tale that I'd been—available to almost any man, mostly to get his own back because I had broken it off with him.' She saw Thad's quick frown and said, 'I think he was also protecting his own reputation by smearing mine. He'd been drinking, and indiscreet, but gossip about me and *men* was less damaging than gossip concerning *him* and me. He covered himself and punished me. When he offered me the job he said he was sorry, and wanted to make it up to me. I thought that, like me, he'd completely got over whatever happened between us years ago. I certainly had no feelings left for him.'

She paused, trying to fathom from Thad's face if he believed her so far, and braced herself for the difficult part. His hard face and watchful eyes gave her no encouragement, but she plunged on:

'The bank had a party, just before Christmas. Ross offered to bring me home afterwards—it was quite late. I didn't realise until he got into the fresh air that he'd drunk a lot. He seemed aware of its effect on him, too, when we got here, and he asked if I would make him some coffee. He lives out of town, you know, and it seemed a sensible request.'

'So you invited him in,' said Thad, as she paused, trying to think how to go on.

'I suppose it was stupid,' she admitted, remembering that Bret had certainly thought so. 'But he had never made a hint of a pass, and he wasn't very drunk, just a little dizzy, I think.'

'Go on.' Thad's expression became a little grim.

'I brought him in the front door, and as we passed the bedroom I realised I'd left the light on—the dressing-table light. I went in to switch it off, telling him to go into the lounge. But he didn't. He followed me.'

She shivered a little, remembering the smile of triumph on Ross's face as he shut the bedroom door and surveyed her across the room. While she stood frozen by the dressing table, cursing her own stupidity, he had been looking around the room, finally commenting on its decor, his gaze lingering on the inviting turned-down bed with its lilac sheets that had been a wedding present from Vanessa's sister, and the matching nightgown she had laid out before she left, earlier.

'I always made the bed ready and put out my nightgown if I was going to be late in,' she explained to Thad. 'When I was alone, it made the homecoming seem less lonely, somehow. He—he picked up the gown and started looking at it, and I tried to get past him to the door, but he was too quick. He grabbed me and pushed me down on the bed. For a few minutes I was frightened, but I fought him, and eventually he let me go. At first he seemed to think I was pretending to be coy, but I bit his finger, and I think the message sank in.'

A faint glimmering of a grim smile appeared on Thad's face. 'Yes, you have sharp teeth, my little vixen. You left some marks on *me* last night.'

She had, for a short time, fought Thad fiercely last night, until he had shown her how futile that was, simply holding her in his arms until she stopped.

'Well,' she said, 'he didn't get his coffee. I was all ready to resign the following day, but he apologised, apparently sincerely, and promised it wouldn't happen again. I believed him. I didn't know then that he was already writing anonymous letters to you. He must have posted one that morning.'

'*He* was——' Thad's surprise showed in his voice, his suddenly raised eyebrows.

'Yes. I'm positive it was Ross who was responsible for them. He wouldn't admit it when I taxed him with it, but there was a look on his face. You see, he wanted you to think that we were having an affair, because he wanted to make it come true. He had some crazy idea that if he split us up—you and me—he would be able to take up with me where we left off six years ago. He said he was obsessed with me—I didn't believe it at the time, but I do now. I think no one has ever hit at his pride the way I did, by turning him down repeatedly. And I don't think he's quite normal in his mind, especially when he's been drinking. I realised when he kissed me that it was more than just hurt pride. I think he kissed me mainly because he'd seen you at the window and knew you were watching, but the way he did it was—frightening. I told him yesterday morning I was leaving. When he came here last night—well, I've told you about that.'

Thad was still standing there with that watchful, shuttered look.

'You don't believe me,' she sighed. 'Of course. I suppose the evidence against me looks bad, and my explanations must sound fantastic. I'm sorry you can't love me enough to trust my word.' Her voice wavered.

She turned to go out of the room, but his voice stopped her.

'Where are you going?'

'I'm going to pack a bag,' she said. 'I think—for a while at least, I'll stay with my mother. After that, I don't know.'

'You're leaving me?'

'Yes,' she said. 'Please try to understand. I can't live in a marriage without trust.'

'You said you loved me.'

Momentarily she closed her eyes, and her lips compressed. It was unfair to remind her. She was unable to reply.

Thad said, 'Last night—this morning, actually—I decided that no matter what you'd done, I couldn't live without you. I thought—if you could manage to pass over my unforgivable behaviour last night, I would somehow make myself do the same over your lies and your unfaithfulness.'

She turned to face him fully, her eyes blazing angrily. 'I suppose I should thank you for that! But I find it a little difficult to be grateful for your forgiveness for things I never did!'

'I haven't finished,' he said. 'This is in the nature of a confession. I have to tell you the full extent of my arrogant and presumptuous decisions, before I ask *you* to forgive me for being such a blind, crass fool. Of course you were telling the truth all along. If I hadn't been so twisted up with my self-pity and my stupid jealousy, I would have known that your integrity outweighed any amount of so-called evidence.'

Vanessa looked at him with dawning hope in her eyes as he moved and then came to stand before her, not touching her.

His voice soft, he said, 'Last night you showed me what love really is all about. Facing me so bravely with my wounded pride and my misguided fury, and inviting me to do my worst, telling me so defiantly that you could take whatever I dished out. I couldn't help admiring your courage and your pride, even when I set out to smash it and crush it into dust. And when I seemed to have succeeded, I knew who'd really won that battle—you. I hated myself so much for what I had done, I was sure you could only hate me, too, and for ever. But when I dared to wipe away your tears, you didn't shrink away from my touch. I couldn't believe that you'd let me try to comfort you for what I'd done, but you did. You even snuggled against me so trustingly it burned guilt into my very soul. How *could* you let me make love to you after—what had happened before?'

Shakily Vanessa smiled, and put her hand to his cheek. 'Because it *was* love, this time, wasn't it?' she asked.

He caught at her hand and kissed it, then laid it against the scar on his face. 'Oh, *God*, yes!' he said. 'I'd decided, just before, as I told you, that I couldn't leave you or let you go, no matter what. But afterwards, I *knew* that I'd made some ghastly mistake, that no matter what the facts looked like, you'd been telling me the truth. There was no logic in it, but some truths go deeper than logic.'

'So you'd changed your mind about me before I told you how Ross came to be in the bedroom?'

'Yes. I didn't know what the explanation was, but I knew there had to be one. Perhaps I should have stopped you from telling me in the end, but you were obviously bent on spilling the whole story, and determined to tell it at last.' With an experimental smile, he added, 'Besides, I was curious.'

Vanessa's other hand moved up, and she linked both of them behind his neck. 'Purely intellectual curiosity, you mean?' she asked innocently.

His arms came round her waist and pulled her tightly against his body. 'Not entirely, my witch. It helped to clear the air. Do you know, when I came in here this morning, after thinking all this through, I told myself that if you wanted to leave me I wouldn't try to stop you—I didn't have the right. You did say you were leaving?'

'Ages ago. I've changed my mind.'

'You've forgiven me?' His voice was low and husky against her cheek.

'Everything. Have you forgiven *me* for suggesting you wanted to spend the weekend with Celine?'

'I can hardly blame you for that. Not that you had any reason to be jealous. Even if I had aspirations in that direction, she's far too much in love with Ritchie to be interested in any other man.'

'Mmm,' Vanessa murmured doubtfully. Catching his surprised expression, she said, 'I wasn't just being catty, you know, although I admit I was jealous.' She told him what had been said to her at Celine's party.

Thad frowned in surprise. 'Well,' he said, 'Ritchie may be taking advantage of the arrangement, but I doubt very much if Celine is. If you ask me she's playing a waiting game, giving him his freedom and hoping that eventually he'll mature and settle for her alone.'

'Yes,' Vanessa agreed slowly, 'I think you're probably right.' Thinking of Celine, she added, 'By the way, how is she getting home? Haven't you rather left her in the lurch?'

'It's all right, she found someone else before I left. I gave her a very brief and edited version of my reasons for suddenly deciding to come home, and she thoroughly approved. Now, can we leave the subject of Celine, and get back to something much more important?'

'Like what?'

'Like—how much—I love you,' he said, punctuating his words with small kisses on her face before he took her lips, prising them apart with his to allow his tantalising exploration of her mouth.

When at last he released her lips and began nuzzling and nibbling at her earlobe while his hands caressed her back and thighs, Vanessa murmured, 'By the way, did you really kiss Clementina?'

He raised his head to look teasingly into her eyes. 'Once. On her lovely nose. She didn't like me at first, you know. It was in the nature of a sign of truce.'

'I see.'

'While we're on the subject,' he went on, 'what did go on between you and my big brother?'

'Nothing,' she said. 'He took me under his wing, like the big brother that *I* never had, that's all.'

'Purely platonic?' At her forceful nod, he said, 'All

right, I believe you, although it doesn't seem like Bret—or you.'

'It was what I needed at the time,' she explained. 'I guess I could have fallen for him, if he'd ever encouraged it, but he didn't.' Daring to tease, she added, 'So I had to settle for his younger brother.'

Thad's mouth exacted a dizzying, sensual punishment for that, and when he raised his head, he murmured dangerously, 'You were saying?'

'It was a lie!' she whispered. 'I wanted you from the start, when Bret first took me home, but I'd had my fingers burnt once, and I was afraid of you.'

His hands moving on her, his lips exploring her neck and throat, he said softly, 'Bret never did this? or this?'

'No,' she whispered, and again, 'No.'

His hand rested over her fast-beating heart as he asked, 'Are you wearing anything under this silk thing?'

On a breathless little laugh, she said, 'No.'

His hands were verifying it as he smiled down into her eyes, and he said, 'If I suggested going back to bed, would you say no?'

She smiled back at him, her eyes languorous with love, and gave him the answer that he wanted.

Take
these
4
best-selling
novels
FREE
Harlequin Presents
ANNE HAMPSON
gates of steel
Harlequin Presents
ANNE MATHER
sweet revenge
Harlequin Presents
VIOLET WINSPEAR
devil in a silver room
Harlequin Presents
JANET DAILEY
no quarter asked